The Phantom's
DARK
FORCE

Moody Adams

The Phantom's
DARK
FORCE

Moody Adams

The Olive Press
A division of Midnight Call Ministries
West Columbia, SC

ISBN 0-937422-47-9

Published in the United States by
The Olive Publishing
West Columbia, South Carolina 29170 U.S.A.

Manufactured in the United States of America

Cover design by Robby McRight

The Scripture quotations in this book are taken from the *King James* Version of the Bible with these changes for clarity to young readers:
Pronouns for Christ's name are capitalized, references to God's Word and Scripture are capitalized, Saviour=Savior, dishonereth=dishonors, ye = you, thou = you, thy = your, shalt = shall, thee = you, wast = were, hast = have, walketh = walks, shouldest = should, gavest = gave, saith = said or says, doth = does, honour=honor, shew=show, armour=armor, leaveth=left, mine=my, whom=who, labour=labor, "est" and "st" on the end of words is dropped, "eth" and "th" on the end of words is changed to "s."

Books are available in quantity for promotional or premium use. Write to: Director of Special Sales, 4694 Platts Springs Road, West Columbia, S.C. 29170 for information on discounts and terms or call 803-755-0733.

02/25/01

Jason,
I hope this simple
Book will answer
Some of the questions
you have. Believe
in something; are you
will fall for anything.
We are always here
for you & Braxton.
We pray for
You & We
love you,
Brenda &
Pell

For Paul Adams

my son, who has inspired me and taught me
not to give up when things do not come easy.

And for Betty Adams, my wife of 51 years
who has put in so many days and nights helping
prepare this book.

And for the youth of this nation, seeking to find
the reason for evil and the power to overcome it.

CONTENTS:

INTRODUCTION

When Bill Moyers interviewed George Lucas before the release of *Star Wars: Episode 1*, he said, "One explanation for the popularity of *Star Wars* when it appeared is that by the end of the 1970s, the hunger for spiritual experience was no longer being satisfied sufficiently by the traditional vessels of faith."

Lucas responded, "I put the Force into the movie in order to try to awaken a certain kind of spirituality in young people—more a belief in God than a belief in any particular religious system. I wanted to make it so that young people would begin to ask questions about the mystery. Not having enough interest in the mysteries of life to ask the question, 'Is there a God or is there not a God?'—that is for me the worst thing that can happen. I think you should have an opinion about that. Or you should be saying, "I'm looking. I'm very curious about this, and I am going to continue to look until I can find an answer, and if I can't find an answer, then I'll die trying." I think it's important to have a belief system and to have faith."[1]

Star Wars does get people thinking about the supernatural. The story parallels the theme of the Bible, a struggle between the supernatural evil Force and the supernatural good Force. George Lucas said the way he prepared for producing the *Star Wars* movies: "I basically worked out a general theory for the Force, and then I played with it...The real essence was to try to deal with the Force but not to be too specific about it. The Force has two halves: Ashla, the good, and Bogan, the paraforce of evil."[2]

Star Wars presents life as a constant struggle with the dark Force. Likewise, the Bible paints life as a struggle with the "rulers of the darkness:" "For we wrestle not against flesh and blood, but against principalities, against powers, against the rulers of the darkness of this world, against spiritual wickedness in high places" (Ephesians 6:12). Star Wars gives insights into how some are swept away by the evil Empire, while others stand in victory against it.

The movie series also gives tremendous lessons in personal victory over the trials and temptations of the dark Force. The story closed with an exciting climax which closely parallels the Bible's prophecy.

In Star Wars, George Lucas seeks to lead people to question the existence of God and to move them to seek Him. In this book I am presenting answers to the big questions about God and a way to personally know Him through Jesus Christ.

*The show apparently taps into yearnings
for a transporting sensory and mystical experience: in a word, for magic.*
—Time

Chapter 1
THE FORCE
IS NO FANTASY

It was the year 3,300 A.D. and there was trouble in the galaxy. While the *Star Wars* planets were crowned with futuristic droids and spacecraft, they were plagued by the ancient evils of hatred and war. The first three movies, *Episodes IV-VI* recorded the story of a young farm boy, Luke Skywalker, and his war against the dark Force of Darth Vader. The prequel, *Episode I—The Phantom Menace*, takes us back 30 years to the time of Qui-Gon Jinn and the battles with the dark Force of Darth Maul.

The *Star Wars* story has gripped hearts around the world because it explores the world of evil. It explains the very terrors that are troubling us in the present world. The series delves into the conflicts between good and evil which we face. And, more important, *Star Wars* gives lessons on winning over the impossible evils we face.

Rick McCallum, the producer of *Episode 1*, thinks he knows another secret of the most successful series in film history: "The story is meaningful," he says, "simply because there's an age of longing that people go through. That's what the story is about: longing and yearning. We ask ourselves, 'What's next? Can I be the person I want to be?' For some, the dream comes true."[3]

Star Wars has an even deeper appeal: "The show apparently taps into yearnings for a transporting sensory and mystical experience: in a word, for magic," as *Time* magazine said of another Phantom production; *The Phantom of the Opera* stage play.[4] *Star Wars* is also a mystical experience, dealing with the supernatural—dealing with the Force.

Skeptics deny the Force

Han Solo, the dashing *Star Wars* pilot who appears in *Episodes IV-VI*, refused to believe in the supernatural Force. He told young Luke Skywalker, "Hokey religions and ancient weapons are no match for a good blaster at your side, kid."

Luke replied: "You don't believe in the Force, do you?"

Han said: "Kid, I've flown from one side of this galaxy to the other. I've seen a lot of strange stuff, but I've never seen anything to make me believe there's one all-powerful Force controlling everything. There's no mystical energy field that controls my destiny."

Ben Kenobi, former Commander of the White Legions, smiled at his skepticism. Han said, "It's all a lot of simple tricks and nonsense."

Then Ben said: "Your eyes can deceive you. Don't trust them." He tells Luke to try the Force. He makes a ball shoot up in the air. Ben says: "You see, you can do it." But

Han Solo still refused to believe. He says: "I call it luck."

Ben Solo is like some people in the present world. They refuse to believe in anything supernatural. The idea of a Devil is rejected. Not only refusing to believe, they even ridicule the idea. Cartoonists draw the Devil as a comic figure in a red union suit. Jokers tell ministers who have just presented a message on the Devil, "Pastor you sure were full of your subject today." Even many serious preachers talk about God, but keep quiet about Satan: it seems they would as soon talk about a flat earth.

But the wisest of men have believed in the unseen world of the evil Force. Socrates was certain he was guided and inspired by his "daemon," or demon. Plato said, "All the intercourse in conversation between gods and men is carried on by the mediation of "demons." The educated Romans called their demons "numina." The Teutons labeled them "incubi." The Chinese lit bon fires and developed fire crackers to chase demons away. The learned Greeks kept quiet when passing cemeteries lest they anger the dark spirits of the dead resting in the graves.

The great Bible teacher, Dr. F. J. Huegel called for everyone to think about where all the evil in our world is coming from: "There is nothing our age so needs as a re-valuation of evil. The Force of terrific circumstances which threaten to wreck civilization and which are causing men's hearts to fail them for fear...demand a fresh investigation of the springs of evil. If in other days it mattered little whether the Biblical definition of evil was to be taken seriously or not—today I must know, for as never before, the foundations of human welfare are being threatened. The conflict has become so fierce, so maddening, so desperate that—well, one would just like to know who or what it is we are fighting....Is evil simply a tendency of the heart of man, bent on wickedness, or are we to take seriously the Scriptural Devil? Is evil nothing more than a lack of development—the stage, as some would have us believe, in which man finds himself in evolution's process, or does this world actually lie as St. John in his first epistle states, 'in the evil one'? Is the primary source of evil a supernatural being who hates God and who is bent on turning man against Him so that he may capture for himself the devotion of men; or is it nothing more than man's own greed for self?"

The depth of evil

Star Wars shows the horrible depth of wickedness. Darth Vader pushed a button and destroyed the peaceful planet Alderaan. It was a beautiful island suspended in a sea of Cirrus Methane, where the good Princess Leia Organa, a member of the Alderaan Senate and leader of the New Republic, had lived. The evil Darth Vader, Lord of Alderaan, destroyed the planet and all its people as easily as a person swats a fly.

This dark story is told in *Star Wars: A New Hope*. Princess Leia is held prisoner on the Death Star spaceship. Darth Vader tried to get her to tell where the Rebels were hiding. She told them they were on the planet Dantooine. But, Tarkin said, "Dantooine is too remote to make an effective demonstration. But don't worry. We will deal with your Rebel friends soon enough."

Leia cried, "No!"

Inside the Death Star blast chamber a voice commanded, "Commence primary ignition." A light panel was switched on. Then a hooded Imperial soldier pulls some levers. A huge beam of light shot out of a cone-shaped area and focused into a single laser beam aimed at Alderaan. The peaceful, green planet is blown into dust. All life is destroyed; every man woman and child disappears.

Later, when Han and Luke search for Alderaan, Han said, "That's what I'm trying to tell you, kid. It ain't there. It's been totally blown away." He realized it has been destroyed by the evil Empire. The planet is gone forever.

Like the dark Force of *Star Wars*, the depths of Satan's power on our planet goes to terrible depths. What Hitler did was as wicked as Darth Vader in the *Star Wars* movies. Walk the halls of Hitler's concentration camps like Dachau and Auschwitz. See some of the prisons where gas chambers murdered six million Jews, where meat hooks transported their bodies, and where giant ovens cremated the remains.

The Jews have been persecuted here just like the Rebels in *Star Wars*. Stop in Israel's museum of the Holocaust and try to explain the lampshade there made from the skin of a Jew. Look at the hundreds of blood-curdling pictures on display. Then answer why the Nazi's would not only commit such horrendous acts, but then would take hundreds of photographs to preserve the morbid memories that delighted them?

Some wars can be explained in terms of the natural. They can be blamed on retaliation, misunderstandings, and blatant greed. But not Dark Vader's attacks, nor Hitlers. The issues are clearly sinister—beyond all reason. Hitler's Germany believed the Aryans were superior to all other races and were destined to rule the world. A super race was to be bred. All Jews were to be exterminated. These atrocities were not carried out by a barbaric, unenlightened jungle tribe; they were enacted by the educated, cultured, religious, and advanced society of Germany.

Just as the Skywalker family was persecuted for giving birth to Luke Skywalker, who had the power to overcome the evil Emperor, Satan has persecuted the Jews for giving birth to Jesus, who had the power to defeat him.

The breadth of evil

From the beginning to the end, the *Star Wars* film series includes a broad cast of evil characters. In the beginning of *Phantom Menace, Episode I*, the evil Darth Maul, the Dark Lord of Sith, is in vicious pursuit of Queen Amidala. In the end there is a horrifying war. *Time* magazine describes it as "the climactic battle between the ragged forces of good and the minions of the dark side."[5]

In *Star Wars: A New Hope*, an Imperial Star Destroyer is chasing a tiny silver spacecraft trying to kill its passengers. Star Destroyer pursues the enemy. Hundreds of deadly laserbolts shoot from the evil Emperor's craft. As an explosion rocked the good Rebel's ship, Threepio cried, "We're doomed."

The final edition, *Return of the Jedi*, ends with a massive war to destroy all who oppose the wicked rule of the Imperial Forces.

In between, the story centers on the murderous efforts of the Empire. Its resources are poured into building killer spaceships. Its energies go into training troops to kill. *Star Wars* is just what the title says, war after war among the stars. All are instigated by the continuously evil dark Force.

Like *Star Wars*, human history is a tale of blood and war. It began when the first family's son, Cain, murdered his brother. It will end with nations murdering nations at Armageddon. In between, are thousands of years of hatred, murder, and wars. All man's progress has not been able to stop the Force of evil.

The senselessness of evil

The murder of the big burly Jawas shows how senseless evil is. These animal creatures were certainly no threat to the Imperial army. Yet, for no good reason the stormtroopers of the dark Force butcher the creatures. Luke Skywalker was wiped out by this senseless killing: "Why would Imperial troops want to slaughter Jawas?" There is no reasonable answer. The forces of the Emperor were set upon killing even when there was no sense to be made of it.

The depths of evil cannot be explained apart from a supernatural dark Force. Take the example of the senseless conduct of a drunk. Watch men get stoned and lose control. Then see what happens. Do they ever stagger down to the home of an old couple and cut their grass? Do drunks ever go out and paint a widow's house? No. They curse. They fight. They wreck a car. They rob a convenience store.

What sensible reason can be given for the drunk's conduct? Logic demands that if a man loses control and no outside force is acting upon him, fifty percent of the time he should do something good and fifty percent of the time something evil. But it doesn't work that way. An outside force is relentlessly working upon people. The Bible instructs, "Be sober, be vigilant; because your adversary the devil, as a roaring lion, walks about, seeking who he may devour" (I Peter 5:8-9). In other words, stay sober, because if we get drunk we'll lose control and when we lose control, the dark Force will take over our lives.

Proof of the Phantom Force can be found in our own life. If we stop and think we have done things we swore we would never do; things we look back on with regret. But we know we did them. Many times we have asked ourselves, "Why did I do such a stupid thing?" There is no answer, if there is no dark Force.

The most crushing evidence of the evil Force in the present world is the senseless crimes and unprovoked killings of the innocent. Why are totally strangers gunned down in drive-by shootings for no good reason? Why do youth walk

into a school room and slaughter their classmates with automatic weapons? Why do parents drown their own children? Jesus explained these in terms of an unseen Force, "You are of your father the devil, and the lusts of your father you will do. He was a murderer from the beginning" (John 8:44).

The dark Force walked
the corridors of Stanford University

Han Solo refused to believe in the dark Force, as do skeptics today. But, these skeptics would have trouble explaining what happened in the chapel of Stanford University. Here is the documented account of this diabolical event.

At 11:30 P.M. on October 12, 1974, nineteen-year-old Bruce Perry interrupted his studies to walk across the Stanford campus to mail some letters. His bride of six months, Arlis, told him she was going over to the chapel to pray before it closed. They agreed to meet a few minutes later back at their apartment. Neither knew the Devil was lurking in the shadows of the sprawling California campus.

At 11:50 P.M. Arlis pulled open the massive chapel doors and joined two others in a silent session of prayer. At midnight the other worshipers saw Arlis praying as they left.

At 12:10 A.M. security guard Steve Crawford shouted, "We're closing for the night. If anyone is here, you'll have to leave." There was no answer. Investigator Maury Terry wrote, "Crawford shut the doors, locked them, and walked away—leaving Arlis Perry alone with the devil in the house of God."

At 12:15 Bruce Perry stood in front of the chapel's locked doors. He had decided to walk over and meet his young bride and was puzzled he had missed her.

At 3:00 A.M., failing to find Arlis anywhere, Bruce called security police and reported his wife was missing.

At 5:30 A.M. Steve Crawford opened the chapel and searched until he found Arlis' body. A witness related in the book, *The Ultimate Evil*, that the sight was "ritualistic and Satanic." Arlis' body was laying near the spot she had prayed. Her legs were spread apart. She was nude from the waist down. A candle, which had been placed in the center of her chest, protruded through a tear in her blouse. Another candle, 30 inches long, had been rammed into her vagina. Arlis had been beaten and choked. The handle of an ice pick protruded from her head. It had been driven into her skull behind her left ear.

They buried Arlis in her hometown, Bismark, North Dakota. The Rev. Hammerton-Kelly referred to Arlis as a "member of the Body of Christ who was cutoff as she prayed." "Violence," the minister said, "has swept to the very altar of God." Police found this note scribbled in a book about Satanism; "Arlis Perry: hunted, stalked, and slain. Followed to California."[6] The note was written by David Berkowitz, the celebrated Son of Sam killer, who terrorized New York City. Thanks to the persistence of investigator Maury Terry the truth finally came out. Arlis Perry was killed by a group of Satanists called "The Process." Killers Charles Manson and "Son of Sam" David Berkowitz both have links to this group that killed an innocent stranger. Arlis' death makes no sense apart from some outside force acting upon the killers.

The conclusion

Dan Crawford's famous rhyme says:

"And so they've voted the Devil out,
And of course, the Devil's gone;
But simple folk would like to know
Who carries his business on."

Han Solo can deny the existence of the evil Force all he wishes. But he can give no logical explanation for the bloody slaughter the evil Force inflicts upon innocent people, except "luck"—"bad luck."

I once asked a psychiatrist, "Do you believe in supernatural devils and demons?" She replied, "I do not want to. But I have files full of cases you cannot explain in terms of the natural. It appears some outside evil Force has to be acting on them.

Jesus Christ declared man has a supernatural enemy and that this was one reason He came to earth: "For this purpose the Son of God was manifested, that he might destroy the works of the devil" (I John 3:8).

Without the good Force working in Ben and Luke, they never could have defeated Darth Vader. Without the good Force of Jesus Christ men cannot defeat the Devil. But, through Him there is victory. Paul said, Jesus has rescued "us from the power of darkness, and has translated us into the kingdom of his dear Son" (Colossians 1:13).

All the brutality, all the senseless killings, all the wars
that would stain the planets with blood, and all the evil
that would terrorize mankind came from
the innocent Anachin Skywalker.

Chapter 2
BORN IN REBELLION

Evil springs from strange sources. The *Star Wars'* three
"prequels" take the audiences on a journey to the beginning of
evil. *Episode 1—The Phantom Menace*, flashes back to the
story of a blue eyed nine-year-old boy in the desert city of Tatooine named Anakin Skywalker. Having a natural talent for
working with machinery, Anakin was a bright young me-
chanic with a dream of becoming a star pilot. The $115 mil-
lion epic, flashes back a whole generation to trace the story of
Anakin. The audience watches him pursue his goals and
struggle with his fears during a dark crisis in his galaxy. The
adventurous Anakin rises to the exciting heights of becoming
a Jedi knight.

But ultimately, Anakin surrendered to the dark Force.
Ben, a leader of the good Force said, "When I first knew him,
your father was already a great pilot. But I was amazed how

strongly the Force was with him. I took it upon myself to train him as a Jedi. I thought that could instruct him just as well as Yoda. I was wrong." Years later he would boast to Ben, "When I left you, I was but the learner; now I am the master." Ben replied, "Only a master of evil, Darth."

Virtue gives birth to a villain

Anakin Skywalker, who was once a bright young boy, became the terror of the dark Force—the wicked Darth Vader. All the brutality, all the senseless killings, all the wars that would stain the planets with blood and all the evil that would terrorize mankind were directed by a man, who had once been a nice lad—Anakin Skywalker.

In an even more bizarre, but strikingly similar story, the evil Force of our world is centered in a creature who was once an angel named Lucifer. More than just another angel, he was the wisest of Heaven's celestial beings. The Bible says: "Thus said the Lord GOD; You seal up the sum, full of wisdom" (Ezekiel 28:12).

Lucifer was beautiful beyond description: "You have been in Eden the garden of God; every precious stone was your covering, the sardius, topaz, and the diamond, the beryl, the onyx, and the jasper, the sapphire, the emerald, and the carbuncle, and gold" (Ezekiel 28:13). Just to look at Lucifer was to experience beauty. His stunning skin was of dazzling diamonds, emeralds, sapphires and gold.

To hear Lucifer breathe was like listening to the sound of beautiful music: "The workmanship of your tabrets and of your pipes was prepared in you in the day that you were created" (Ezekiel 28:13).

Lucifer was the highest of God's celestial beings: "You art the anointed cherub that covers; and I have set you so: you were upon the holy mountain of God; you have walked up and down in the midst of the stones of fire" (Ezekiel 28:14).

From this beautiful, covering cherub flowed all the evil in the present world.

The rebellion

Ben explained the fall of Anakin to his son Luke Skywalker: "Your father was seduced by the dark side of the Force. He ceased to be Anakin Skywalker and became Darth Vader. When that happened, the good man who was your father was destroyed."

In an interview regarding the movie, producer George Lucas explained the story this way: "I wanted the father to be Darth Vader, but I also wanted a father figure. So I created Ben as the other half. You have one who is the light half and one who is the dark half...the positive and the negative. This sort of gave a twist to the whole story...Moving in the area of the Force and then trying to describe it, trying to come up with a name for it, trying to describe this other existence, I didn't want to use God or any of those kinds of connotations. Even though I called it the Force of this and the Force of that in the beginning, I eventually shorthanded it just to the Force."[7]

Lucifer was not just good like Anakin Skywalker. In fact, for a long time he was perfect: "You were perfect in your ways from the day that you were created, untill iniquity was found in you" (Ezekiel 28:15).

How does a great Heavenly Prince, perfect in every way, full of wisdom, shrouded in beauty, sounding forth music in the Celestial Courts become the Devil? What was the iniquity that brought down the great Lucifer? The Bible says this angel sinned because his heart was lifted up with pride: "You have sinned: therefore I will cast you as profane out of

the mountain of God: and I will destroy you, O covering cherub, from the midst of the stones of fire. Your heart was lifted up because of your beauty, you have corrupted your wisdom by reason of your brightness" (Ezekiel 28:16,17). He thought himself too pretty to be subject to anyone, even God.

Lucifer's pride dirtied the dwelling of God and brought himself down: "You have defiled your sanctuaries by the multitude of your iniquities" (Ezekiel 28:18).

The Bible says, "How art you fallen from heaven, O Lucifer, son of the morning! how art you cut down to the ground, which did weaken the nations! For you have said in your heart, I will ascend into heaven, I will exalt my throne above the stars of God: I will sit also upon the mount of the congregation, in the sides of the north: I will ascend above the heights of the clouds; I will be like the most High. Yet you shall be brought down to hell, to the sides of the pit" (Isaiah 14:12-15).

Pride was Lucifer's downfall. Discontented with being just a covering cherub, he said, "I will be like the most high"—"I will be god". His proud ambition erupted into a war: "There was war in heaven: Michael and his angels fought against the dragon; and the dragon four and his angels, And prevailed not; neither was their place found any more in heaven. And the great dragon was cast out, that old serpent, called the Devil and Satan which deceived the whole world: he was cast out into the earth, and his angels were cast out with him" (Revelation 12:7-9). Lucifer failed to capture the throne of God, was thrown out of heaven, and evil was born.

Some people ask why God would create evil. Their reasoning is if He is all loving he would not have created evil. If He is all-powerful He could certainly stop evil. So why do people suffer from evil? The Bible's answer is very clear. God did not create evil. He created a perfect angel named Lucifer:

"You were perfect in your ways from the day you were created" (Ezekiel 28:15). God did not create a Devil, but a cherub, "full of wisdom and perfect in beauty." But God gave His perfect creature a free will. Just as Anakin Skywalker could choose between the good Force and the dark Force, so could Lucifer. He chose to rebel against God: "You were perfect...till iniquity was found in you." Evil was born the day the angel Lucifer chose to rebel and overthrow the throne of God. As an unknown poet wrote:

> "I had ambition,
>   The sin by which the angels fell.
> I climbed up step by step
>   And ascended into hell."

The evil hierarchy

Star Wars' Darth Maul and Darth Vader were not alone in their rebellion. They recruited massive forces. A massive army loyal to the dark Force was involved in *The Phantom Menace's* final battle scene. In *The Return of the Jedi*, there were thousands of soldiers in tight formation that filled the mammoth docking bay of Vader's ship, Death Star. Vader also had an evil hierarchy—a group of powerful personal advisers. They appear in flaming red dress, a sharp contrast to the black attire of Vader.

Nilo Rodislamero, who did a lot of the design work on the *Star Wars* movies, explained why these high-leveled advisers appeared dressed in red: "On *Jedi,* one of the most exciting things from a design point of view was the advisers who surround the Emperor. I spent a lot of time trying to figure out what they might look like because I thought it was important that through them you might understand what the Emperor's world is like. Coming from a Catholic background, I sort of made a joke, and that's why they look like bishops. So they wear red, and they have elaborate headgear."[8]

Likewise, Lucifer was not alone in his rebellion. He used his cunning wisdom to get many other angels to join him: "For God spared not the angels that sinned, but cast them down to hell, and delivered them into chains of darkness, to be reserved unto judgment" (II Peter 2:4). The Phantom Prince became the ruler of a great hierarchy of spiritual beings including: "principalities," "powers," "rulers of the darkness of this world," and "wicked spirits" (Ephesians 6:12).

A figurative passage in Revelation indicates a third of the angels in heaven banned with Lucifer. They were cast out of heaven and became fallen angels, or "demons:" "There appeared another wonder in heaven; and behold a great red dragon, having seven heads and ten horns, and seven crowns upon his heads. And his tail drew the third part of the stars of heaven, and did cast them in the earth" (Revelation 12:3-4). Jesus referred to the unholy army as "the devil and his angels" (Matthew 25:41).

Evil rules in power

Darth Vader, like Darth Maul before him, embodied evil. He wore black clothes and a black shield over his face. And his heart was even blacker. In the film, *The Empire Strikes Back*, Vader killed Admiral Ozzel because he failed to sneak up on the Rebels. Vader replaced Ozzel with Admiral Piett, before choking Ozzel to death for that one small failure.

The evil Darth Vader ruled with great power. He headed a gigantic army of fierce stormtroopers. He traveled in the awesome, giant ship Star Destroyer. Five Imperial Star Destroyers were with him. These six ships were surrounded by a huge convoy of smaller spacecraft. One blast of his laser had destroyed a planet.

But Vader has greater power than that of the laser guns, spaceships, and troops. He has supernatural power. When Motti boast of their army's fire power, Vader tells him "The ability to destroy a plant is insignificant next to the power of the Force." Motti replies, "Don't try to frighten us with your sorcerer's ways, Lord Vader. Your sad devotion to that ancient religion has not helped you conjure up the stolen data tapes or given you clairvoyance enough to find the Rebels' hidden fort." Then Vader shows his power by putting a spell on Motti. Vader's spell made him choke and turn blue.

Earth's evil Phantom also, rules with tremendous power. He is called "Beelzebub" (the Prince of Demons), the "God of this Age," and "the Prince of the Power of the Air." He reigns in power over this world.

Dr. F. J. Huegel said, "The primary source of evil is not man—it does not spring from his pride nor his greed nor his ignorance nor his lust. When man appeared, the Prince of Darkness...was already on deck."

People must understand they have a powerful enemy present in this world. The Devil is not confined to hell. He is walking the crowded streets of our cities, prowling the corridors of our schools, and creeping about our homes. We do not have to raise the Devil. He is right with us every moment.

Knowing the enemy

The people of the good Force in *Star Wars* knew they were fighting the supernatural dark Force. There was no misunderstanding about this. We will never win the battle of life unless we know who our enemy is. We must constantly be aware that the enemy is not bad luck or bad people. It is the fallen angel Lucifer. We must clearly label him as our real enemy.

When friends say things that deeply hurt us, we must remember they are not our enemy and say, "This is Satan's attack."

When members of your family break your heart, we need to remember they are not our enemy and say, "This is the evil Force at work."

When senseless, bloody crimes fill the evening news, let us remember this is not the fault of flesh and blood and say, "This is the dark Force's menace."

When we visit the cemeteries containing the bodies of many slain in war, we must say, "This is the Devil's work."

For a thousand generations the Jedi Knights
were the guardians of peace and justice in the
Old Republic. Before the dark times, before the Empire. "
—Ben Kenobi

Chapter 3
WHAT IT WAS LIKE
BEFORE THE DARK TIMES

The dark Force can steal the finest paradise and turn it into a hell. Ben described what the Galaxy was like before the dark times; before the *Star Wars* began. Then it was a relative heaven on earth: "For over a thousand generations the Jedi Knights were the guardians of peace and justice in the Old Republic." Before the dark times, before Darth Maul and the Empire. Things were good in those days. Then the dark Force stole paradise.

The fantasy world of *Star Wars* reflects what has happened in the present world. Man, created in a splendid paradise of beauty, originally had no crime to fear. People felt no pain. God walked in blissful fellowship with mankind. Death could not enter this land of splendor. But suddenly paradise was shattered. Man fell and was driven out into a world of tears and pain; of suffering and death. Paradise was replaced by a world of hospitals, orphanages, wars and cemeteries where God was no more to be seen.

The fallen Lucifer triumphed in Eden and left man, the crown of creation, in ruins. "The fallen Prince, once the Son of the Morning, introducing himself into God's Fair Garden to wrest from the Hands of his Creator, man, and to plunge him into the night of alienation from his Father and his God. A darker picture could not be conceived...The Crown of Creation snatched from God's Hand and made to serve diabolical purposes," writes Dr. Huegle.

The test

In *Star Wars* the characters are constantly tested by choices between good and evil. Laurent Bouzereau, who worked on the movies, wrote, "It was decided that learning the ways of the Force had to be a constant struggle for Luke and that he would always have to prove himself. In regard to the dark side of the Force, the story meeting transcripts suggest that although one can't see it, it should be the real villain of the story. In his training Luke discovers the roots of the evil Force. The danger, the jeopardy is that Luke will become Vader, will be taken over. He has to fight the bad side and learn to work with the good side."[9]

In the present world, God created a perfect man and put him in a magnificent paradise—Eden. Man had no knowledge of evil. His conscience had never been stained by one single misdeed. His Paradise was conditional on only one thing—that he not eat of forbidden fruit: "And the Lord God took the man, and put him into the garden of Eden to dress it and to keep it. And the Lord God commanded the man, saying, Of every tree of the garden you may freely eat: But of the tree of the knowledge of good and evil, you shall not eat of it: for in the day that you eat thereof you shall sure die" (Genesis 2:15-17).

God asked only one small thing of man, not to eat of one tree. If he ate the fruit it would show rebellion against God. If he did not eat it would show trust in God. God permitted Satan into the garden to see if he could win the affections of Adam and get him to eat the forbidden fruit.

Why did God allow this? Why would He risk man's fall and subsequent death? Simply to find out if man really loved Him. God had created man to love him. When a young man came to Jesus and asked, "Master, which is the great commandment in the law? Jesus said unto him, You shall love the Lord your God with all your heart, and with all your soul, and with all your mind. This is the first and great commandment" (Matthew 22:36-38). The first of the Ten Commandments is: "You shall have no other gods before me" (Exodus 20:3). God wants to be our first love. This is why He created us.

But discovering whether man loved God required two things: man must have a free will so he could choose to love or not to love, and man must have another suitor to test his affections. If God had not given man freedom to choose, he would not have been capable of love. He would have been a mere puppet on a string, or a ventriloquist dummy. For man to love God, he had to have the ability to choose. Also, for man to prove his love for God he must be put to the test, an attractive seducer must be allowed to try him.

Suppose a man and his wife were marooned alone on an island. There is an abundance of fruit and fish. The island is beautiful beyond words. The husband has no TV to watch, no trips to take with the fellows, and no ball games to attend. He gives all of his attention and affection to his wife. He tells her of his love. It is wonderful for three weeks. Then one day as he embraces her and tells her he loves her, the wife begins to think, "Of course he says he loves me. I am the only woman on the island. But, suppose some blonde drifts up one day. Will he still show me such affection?" Doubts possess her. She doesn't know whether her husband really means it, and she never will. Her husband's words and acts of affection become clouded by doubt. The island paradise is turned into a hell on earth.

Likewise, God can never know whether man loves him as long as there is no one else to bid for his affections. The Creator must allow Lucifer to enter the garden. If he can win man's affections, the Devil wins. If he can't, God knows man loves him and God wins.

The mistake

In *The Empire Strikes Back*, Luke declares, "I feel the Force!" Ben replies, "But you cannot control it. This is a dangerous time for you, when you will be tempted by the dark side of the Force...It is you and your abilities the Emperor wants." The evil Emperor wants Luke. He plots to turn him to the Dark Side.

Likewise, earth's fallen Phantom, Lucifer, is permitted to come down into the world to try and seduce Adam and Eve. Jesus said, "I beheld Satan as lightning fall from heaven" (Luke 10:18). This fall landed Lucifer in man's paradise: "You have been in Eden the garden of God" (Ezekiel 28:13). He enters the garden and sets out to turn earth's first couple to the Dark Side. The Devil, an invisible spirit being with no body of his own, enters the body of a beautiful animal who was "more subtle" than any creature.

He begins his seduction of Eve with a seemingly innocent remark. "And he said unto the woman, Yea hath God said, You shall not eat of every tree of the garden?" (Genesis 3:1) What a loaded statement. It drives a wedge of doubt about whether God really cares for man and raises some powerful questions in Eve's mind: "If God loves me why does he impose any limitation on me? Am I some kind of slave or am I free? Why should I obey someone who would forbid me to do whatever I wish?"

Then, "The woman said unto the serpent, We may eat of the fruit of the trees of the garden: But of the fruit of the tree which is in the midst of the garden, God has said, You shall not eat of it, neither shall you touch it, lest you die. And the serpent said unto the woman, You shall not surely die: For God does know that in the day you eat thereof, then your eyes shall be opened, and you shall be as gods, knowing good and evil" (Genesis 3:2-5). The charge is clear: "God couldn't possibly love you and suppress you as He does. He does not want you to gain all the knowledge He possesses. Obviously, He is jealous, wanting to prevent you from ever being His equal. So he suppresses you and refuses to allow you the knowledge that would make you His equal—a God!" (Genesis 3:1).

First, the Devil planted the seed of doubt, then he nourished it to full bloom, convincing the woman Eve, and then Adam to give their trust, obedience, and affections to Lucifer rather than to the God that had created them: "And when the woman saw that the tree was good for food, and that it was pleasant to the eyes, and a tree to be desired to make one wise, she took of the fruit thereof, and did eat, and gave also unto her husband with her; and he did eat" (Genesis 3:6).

And so, man chose not to trust God—to turn his back on his Creator and trust Lucifer. The Devil triumphed. God would not take away man's free will and coerce man to love Him. Rather, man must choose and face the consequences of his choice.

In *Star Wars: A New Hope*, Luke Skywalker saw what evil could do to a person. He had seen Darth Vader, who had been turned into an evil monster by yielding to the dark Force. Luke realized it could happen to him.

The Fall

But, Adam and Eve did not understand. When they took the fruit of disobedience, they believed it would lead to greater freedom, more knowledge, and a happier life. With the eating of the fruit came the belief that they would be changed into gods. They were changed, not into gods but into slaves of "self." The effects were instantaneous. They fell from the lofty plains of loving God to the deep valley of self-centered, self love.

By this one single act, Adam and Eve guaranteed that each of their descendants would be born to love themselves above all else. The Apostle Paul stated this vividly: "We... were by nature the children of wrath, even as others" (Ephesians 2:3).

This meant children would scream and throw temper tantrums when they couldn't have everything they wanted. Teenagers would break the hearts of the parents who had devoted their lives to raising them. Husbands would betray their wives and children for a young woman they found pleasant to the eye. Men would be born with a desire to fight each other in bloody wars: "From whence come wars and fightings among you? come they not hence, even of your lusts that war in your members. You lust, and have not: you kill, and desire to have, and cannot obtain: you fight and war, yet you have not" (James 4:1-2).

Soon Adam and Eve saw the horrid results of their folly. Their son Cain killed his brother Able in a jealous rage: "Not as Cain, who was of that wicked one, and slew his brother. And wherefore slew he him? Because his own works were evil, and his brother's righteous" (I John 3:12). From the dead boy's side came a stream of blood that would run through history. In an ever-widening river, that blood would stain the battlefields of the world.

This explains the existence of evil in the human race. It was not created by God but by a good angel and a good man with free wills who chose to rebel against God. Bible teacher E.C. Jennings said, "God is absolute Good, and only Good. Nothing that is not good could come from such a Source. A sweet fountain may send forth poison; the sun may produce darkness and night sooner than God produce evil in the sense of wickedness. He therefore no more created the devil as such, that is as he now is, than He created man as be now is. No 'liar' or 'murderer' ever sprang from His creative will."

The Loss of Innocence

When the dark Force ended the time of peace in the galaxy, man lost his innocence. Both Ben and Luke experienced guilt and shame. So did Adam and Eve. They took the fruit thinking it would be "pleasant," but immediately were cursed with shame and guilt:

> And the eyes of them both were opened, and they knew that they were naked; and they sewed fig leaves together, and made themselves aprons. And they heard the voice of the LORD God walking in the garden in the cool of the day: and Adam and his wife hid themselves from the presence of the LORD God amongst the trees of the garden. And the LORD God called unto Adam, and said unto him, Where art you? And he said, I heard

your voice in the garden, and I was afraid, because I was naked; and I hid myself. And he said, Who told you that you were naked? Have you eaten of the tree, whereof I commanded you that you should not eat? And the man said, The woman who you gave to be with me, she gave me of the tree, and I did eat. And the LORD God said unto the woman, What is this that you have done? And the woman said, The serpent beguiled me, and I did eat (Genesis 3:7-13).

The foliage that had been a source of shade and beauty became only something to cover their guilt. Man had lost his innocence and had to practice concealment. Inside his heart the ghost of guilt abided, torturing him constantly. With the knowledge of evil comes horrid shame.

Separation from God

When Darth Maul and Darth Vader, chose the dark side, it completely separated them from the good side and everyone on it. Vader was even separated from his own son and daughter and became their bitter enemy.

Adam and Eve were driven out of Paradise and lost their relationship with God. They entered a dark night of total separation from their Creator. The loss of a parent, a mate, or a child is terrible, but the loss of God is beyond the measure of human tears. Adam and Eve lost their God. No more would the Creator of heaven and earth walk with them in the Garden of Paradise. They lost the greatest love ever known. Worse still, all their children would be separated from God: "Being alienated from the life of God" (Ephesians 4:18).

Centuries later, David would cry, "As the hart pants after the water brooks, so pants my soul after you, O God.

My soul thirsts for God, for the living God: when shall I come and appear before God?" (Psalms 42:1-2). David's cry has been that of mankind through the ages. The human race has a thirst that cannot be quenched until a reunion with God occurs.

Paul expressed this longing when he cried, "That I might know Him." Lornie Sanny, the head of the Navigators, called these the five greatest words in the Bible. They aptly express the deepest hunger of the human heart—to know the God we walked with in Eden.

The Curse of Misery

Star Wars is a tale of endless suffering. The dark Force spread pain, war, and misery throughout the planets. Disobedience brought a horrid curse upon the earth.

The same is true for earth's humans. God said, "And unto the woman he said, I will greatly multiply your sorrow and your conception; in sorrow you shall bring forth children" (Genesis 3:16). "Because you have eaten of the tree, of which I commanded you, saying you shall not eat of it: cursed is the ground for your sake; in sorrow shall you eat of it all the days of your life. Thorns also and thistles shall it bring forth to you....In the sweat of your face shall you eat bread" (Genesis 3:17-19).

No more did man just tend a garden and feast on its abundance. He must sweat and toil. The weary workers must know God did not want it to be like this. He gave man the opportunity to live on a perpetual vacation. But man chose to let Lucifer take it all away.

No more did man enjoy the constant happiness he had in paradise: "In sorrow" he ate until he died. When tears run down and life is torture, we must remember this is all the result of man's fall to Satan's seduction.

The Loss of Life

The rise of Evil brought death to the galaxy. In *Star Wars: A New Hope*, Luke's family is killed and the entire population of the planet Alderaan dies. Death reigns.

God told Adam and Eve what the consequences of disobedience would be. "You shall not eat of it, neither shall you touch it, lest you die." No longer did man eat of the tree of life: "Therefore the LORD God sent him forth from the garden of Eden, to till the ground from whence he was taken. So he drove out the man; and he placed at the east of the garden of Eden Cherubims, and a flaming sword which turned every way, to keep the way of the tree of life" (Genesis 3:23-24).

When we stand at the graveside of one we loved, or listen to the doctor's painful words, "it is terminal," we should not ask, "Why? God why?" God is as heartbroken as we are. Death is the work of the Devil who enticed man to sin.

The hope

Despite the triumph of evil over Adam and Eve and the sinful nature of their children, victory is still possible. God foresaw this tragedy and implemented a plan to reclaim people from the Devil. Instantly God gave the promise of a Redeemer: "Her (Eve's) seed; it shall bruise your (Lucifer's) head" (Genesis 3:14-15). God promised that the Devil would be crushed.

Thousands of years later, "When the fulness of the time was come, God sent forth his Son, made of a woman, made under the law, To redeem them that were under the law, that we might receive the adoption of sons" (Galatians 4:4-5).

Luke cried: "Uncle Owen! Aunt Beru! Uncle Owen!"
He searched through the wreckage
of his house for his aunt and uncle.
Then he discovered their smoldering remains.
Luke is so devastated he cannot even speak.
—*Star Wars*: The Final Hope

Chapter 4
ASSAULT ON THE SKYWALKER FAMILY

Evil attacks families in horrible ways. From the first *Star Wars* release, the evil Empire has targeted one family—the Skywalkers. In *Episode I—The Phantom Menace*, Anakin Skywalker is marked by the dark Force. Later he will be turned to the dark side. In *Episode IV—Star Wars: A New Hope*, Luke Skywalker's Uncle Owen and Aunt Beru are destroyed. Luke and his sister, Leila, are attacked by the dark Force from *Episode IV* through the end in *Episode VI*. This family is under assault because they possess the greatest force and are using it for good. To destroy this family would give the dark Force a great, glorious victory.

As it was in *Star Wars*, so it happened in the present

world. Satan targeted a family in the land of Uz. The father lost his wealth, his health, and all his help. His best friends turned against him. His wife gave up on him. His children were killed in an accident. Hopeless depression set in. All the odds were against him. It appeared his family was finished.

Yet he rose from the ashes of defeat to achieve stunning heights of victory. More than two thousand years later his name is a synonym for not giving up. His memory has remained long after all the sports heroes, military masters and political rulers have passed into the sea of oblivion. Not only is he remembered, but his story brings hope and inspiration to hurting families around the world. What did he do that so immortalized his name? His family suffered a fierce attack by the Devil and he overcame the dark Force.

The assailant

The victor's name was Job, a man whose family suffered every conceivable vicious attack by this unseen enemy. Between Satan's victory over Adam and Eve in the first book of the Bible and Satan's defeat in the last book of the Bible, the book of Job gives us the clearest insights into the strategy of Satan. This fallen angel was determined to prove Job did not love God—that God had only bought his affections. And so the Phantom was loosed in this contest for the ages: "Now there was a day when the sons of God came to present themselves before the LORD, and Satan came also among them. And the LORD said unto Satan, Whence come you? Then Satan answered the LORD, and said, From going to and fro in the earth, and from walking up and down in it. And the LORD said unto Satan, Have you considered my servant Job, that there is none like him in the earth, a perfect and an upright man, one that feareth God, and escheweth evil? Then Satan answered the LORD, and said, Doth Job fear God for nought? Have not you made an hedge about him, and about his house, and about all that he has on every side? you have blessed the work of his hands, and his substance is increased in the land. But put forth your hand now, and touch all that he has, and he will curse you to your face. And the LORD said unto Satan, Behold, all that he has is in your power; only upon himself put not forth your hand. So Satan went forth from the presence of the LORD" (Job 1:6-12).

Later, after all of the Devil's initial attack's failed to make Job curse God, the Devil renegotiated the rules: "Again there was a day when the sons of God came to present themselves before the LORD, and Satan came also among them to present himself before the LORD. And the LORD said unto Satan, From whence come you? And Satan answered the LORD, and said, From going to and fro in the earth, and from walking up and down in it. And the LORD said unto Satan, Have you considered my servant Job, that there is none like him in the earth, a perfect and an upright man, one that fears God, and eschews evil? and still he holds fast his integrity, although you moved me against him, to destroy him without cause. And Satan answered the LORD, and said, Skin for skin, yea, all that a man has will he give for his life. But put forth your hand now, and touch his bone and his flesh, and he will curse you to your face. And the LORD said unto Satan, Behold, he is in your hand; but save his life" (Job 2:1-6).

The book of Job makes it unmistakably clear. Satan is the invisible Phantom in charge of the affairs of earth, limited only by the bounds of God's permissive will. The Devil threw a seven-stage attack at Job, but Job did not renounce God, much less curse Him: "In all this did not Job sin with his lips" (Job 2:10). This man won against all odds and gave the world the encouraging expression, "the patience of Job."

His winning secret was his unshakable confidence in God. Unlike Adam and Eve whose faith in God was shaken by the Devil's doubts, Job won. He declared, "Though He slay me, yet will I trust him" (Job 13:15). By faith Job clung to this belief, "He shall deliver you in six troubles: yea, in seven there shall no evil touch you" (Job 5:19). Despite the seven troubles the dark Force cursed Job with, he kept his faith and won.

Trouble number one:
the loss of money

In Star Wars: A New Hope, Luke Skywalker discovered that the evil Empire may have learned where his family lived. He races across the flat landscape in his landspeeder. When he gets to the spot where his home should have been, he discovered there was nothing but smoking holes and scattered debris. His home was gone. His clothes were gone. Everything he had on the planet was gone.

In the ancient land of Uz, Satan stripped Job of his earthly possessions. Enemies from Arabia killed his servants and stole 500 yoke of oxen and 500 she-asses. It was a devastating financial set back.

After this, lightning started a fire that consumed Job's 7,000 sheep and their herdsmen. Then more enemies, the Chaldeans, came in and stole his 3,000 valuable camels. Camels are extremely costly. During a visit to the Middle East, an Arab offered my friend Bill Roberts three camels for his wife Liz. We were told that was an extremely generous offer, considering the great value of the three animals. Bill disagreed. If three is a high price for a wife, imagine the worth of 3,000 camels.

So in one day, Job, one of the richest men in the East, lost all his possessions. But though Job lost his wealth he did not lose his faith. He would one day rise to financial victory when God "gave Job twice as much as he had before" (Job 42:10). No matter how short we may be on money, even if we've lost everything, we can still win. Understand that God is not punishing us. The Devil is attacking us. God is still for us. By faith we, like Job, can win by trusting God.

We must claim this Bible promise, "But my God shall supply all your need according to his riches in glory by Christ Jesus" (Phillipians 4:19).

Trouble number two:
the death of loved ones

Luke cried: "Uncle Owen! Aunt Beru! Uncle Owen!" He searches through the wreckage of his house for his aunt and uncle. Then he discovers their smoldering remains. Luke is so devastated he cannot speak.

Job had ten children. They were all having dinner at his oldest son's house when a tornado struck and killed them all. In one day he lost all his children. But Job kept trusting in the Lord, and later the Lord gave him ten more children. The man had good reason to believe his first ten children were in heaven.

When we lose a loved one, we still have the Lord. "He has said, I will never leave you, nor forsake you" (Hebrews 13:5). No matter how lonely we may be, we can still win just as Job did, by trusting God.

Trouble number three:
the loss of physical well-being

Luke suffered tremendous physical pain and loss. In his early life, as a young would-be Jedi, he was thrown across the room and sent crashing through tables. In the end, Vader's lightsaber came down and cut his right hand off. In between these hurtful events, his life is plagued with pain.

Job, likewise, suffered great pain. He was plagued by horrid "boils from the sole of his foot unto his crown" (Job 2:7). It is bad enough that he could not work, but the pain tortured him unbearably. No ointments, drugs, or sleeping medications, were available to relieve the raging agony. No surgeon's instrument could lance the boils. All Job could do to get relief was to scrape the itching boils with a piece of a broken clay vessel.

In all this pain and suffering, Job refused to give up. After the ordeal, his body healed and his health was restored.

We can win despite health problems. The key is not to give up, and not to blame God, or curse our Creator. This is what the Devil wants. We must keep our faith in God.

Here is the promise of the God who healed Job to those who believe: "The prayer of faith shall save the sick, and the Lord shall raise him up" (James 5:15).

Trouble number four:
the loss of the best supporter

In *Return of the Jedi*, Ben sent Luke to Yoda, the Jedi Master, for training in the use of the good Force. It is a crucial time as Luke prepares for his show-down with the evil Emperor. Yoda is wise and devoted to Luke, but he gives him some bad advice. Luke says he must leave immediately to fight Darth Vader and rescue Han and Leia. Yoda says he must not go because he has not finished his training. When Luke says, "I've got to go to them," Yoda replies, "Decide you must how to serve them best. If you leave now, help them you could. But you would destroy all for which they have fought and suffered." Luke is frozen with discouragement. Yoda's words fill him with gloom. He shakes his head sadly.

Job's wife spoke words just as discouragingly to her suffering, broken husband, "Do you still retain your integrity? curse God, and die" (Job 2:9). It would be extremely difficult to go through the suffering Job faced, even with the support of an encouraging wife. But Job had to go through this alone because his wife gave up. Due to her great love she could not stand to see him going through such suffering. She allowed the Devil to use her mouth to make his appeal: "Curse God, and die."

When those we trust lose faith and give us discouraging advice, we must remember the words come from the dark Force. The Devil, is the one giving us the bad advice. He is our real enemy.

If we have a supportive friend or mate that keeps their confidence in God, we can thank God for them. But if we don't, we can still win just as Job did, by trusting God despite the discouraging words of your best supporter.

When every one else forsakes us, God will be there, "When my father and my mother forsake me, then the LORD will take me up" (Psalms 27:10).

Trouble number five: depression assails the mind

Luke comes to the end of the *Star Wars* drama very discouraged. He has learned that his lifelong enemy, the wicked Darth Vader, is his father. He sees the war with the Emperor's forces going against him. He kneels down to help Artoo, but stops, shakes his head dejectedly and says, "I can't do it. Artoo. I can't go on alone." But somehow he does manage to go on, only to be captured by the Emperor. In a final word of despair he says, "Soon I'll be dead." But he was wrong. The good Force raised Luke up and gave him the victory.

Job also faced hopeless depression. The broken man cried, "Why died I not from the womb? why did I not give up the ghost when I came out of the belly?" (Job 3:11). First his body failed him, then his mind. He forgot there was a God to serve in this world and better things to come in the next world. He sank into hopelessness and depression, thinking he would be better off dead.

But God delivered him from this trouble also and gave him a life filled with joy. Depression does not last forever. God can deliver us in this trouble also, just as he delivered Job.

When we are discouraged and depressed, we must declare our faith in God's promise: "Mine enemies would daily swallow me up: for they be many that fight against me, O you most High. What time I am afraid, I will trust in you" (Psalms 56:2-3).

Trouble number six:
the betrayal of friends

Luke developed a close friend named Biggs, whom he looks up to as a role model. Biggs really liked Luke but gave him some very incorrect, discouraging advice. His good friend told him he was never going to get away from his farm and that he would never get to the academy to become a pilot. Biggs left him. Later as Luke was tinkering around in his garage, he thought about the words of his friend. Frustration got the best of him. Luke says, "It isn't fair. Oh, Biggs is right. I'm never Gonna get out of here!"

Likewise, Job's friends betrayed him with incorrect advice: "All my inward friends abhorred me: and they who I loved are turned against me" (Job 19:19). His friends were the best. They left their homes for seven days to sit with their suffering friend Job. Few men have such friends. Scripture records their devotion: "Now when Job's three friends heard of all this evil that was come upon him, they came every one from his own place; Eliphaz the Temanite, and Bildad the Shuhite, and Zophar the Naamathite: for they had made an appointment together to come to mourn with him and to comfort him. And when they lifted up their eyes afar off, and knew him not, they lifted up their voice, and wept; and they rent every one his mantle, and sprinkled dust upon their heads toward heaven. So they sat down with him upon the ground seven days and seven nights, and none spoke a word unto him: for they saw that his grief was very great" (Job 2:11-13).

They were dumbfounded, speechless at what had befallen Job. The great sheik who was once so rich and famous had become a broken man. What caused this? Job's friends were sure Job was suffering because he was a hypocrite. They did not understand his family was under a Satanic attack. They added to his pain by rebuking him like he was a wicked hypocrite. Where did they get this idea about Job? Elihu speaks to Job of a dream, a vision to awaken him to his sins and keep back his soul from "the pit:" "Behold, in this you art not just: I will answer you, that God is greater than man. Why do you strive against him? for he gives not account of any of his matters. For God speaks once, yea twice, yet man perceives it not. In a dream, in a vision of the night, when deep sleep falls upon men, in slumberings upon the bed; Then he opens the ears of men, and seals their instruction, That he may withdraw man from his purpose, and hide pride from man. He keeps back his soul from the pit, and his life from perishing by the sword" (Job 33:12-18).

They treated Job as a monster who had committed some heinous crime that required God to deal with him so harshly. Satan's piercing accusations of Job, delivered through the mouths of his friends, added immensely to his suffering. But they did not persuade him, despite all the talk about dreams. The Devil, too, can give dreams to man. Job insists they were wrong. And Job is right. God only permitted his suffering. The Devil was the source of his torment. Of course Job over-emphasized his innocence, but this was better than yielding to the charges of hypocrisy. It is far better than embracing the idea that God was punishing him and cursing his Lord for it.

Job chose to let this betrayal shut him up to faith in God. He had no one else to trust. There were no friend to depend upon. Just as Jesus went forward after Judas betrayed Him, Job kept going after his friends betrayed him.

If our friends are faithful and supportive, we can thank God for them. But if they all misunderstand and turn against us, we can still win. Job won without his friends. He won by unbroken faith in God.

Always remember, friends can be depressing: "Our brethren have discouraged our heart...Then I said unto you, Dread not, neither be afraid of them. The LORD your God which goeth before you, he shall fight for you" (Deuteronomy 1:28-30).

Trouble number seven: the approach of death

At the end of *Return of the Jedi*, Luke battled the evil Emperor. Lightening bolts flew from the Emperor's wicked fingers and knock Luke to the floor. As he is laying there writhing in pain, too weak to fight back, the Emperor says, "Now, young Skywalker ...you will die."

In his last Satanic trouble, Job was also brought face to face with his own mortality. Death took him by the hand and whispered, "It is all over for you." It appeared Job was finished. He declared, "Now shall I sleep in the dust; and you shall seek me in the morning, but I shall not be" (Job 7:21).

But faith awoke and Job declared his life will never end, not even at death: "For I know that my redeemer lives, and that he shall stand at the latter day upon the earth: And though after my skin worms destroy this body, yet in my flesh shall I see God" (Job 19:25,26).

We must not quit. We must never give up. We have an unseen enemy working day and night to destroy our families. But, we can win over all of the dark Force's attacks. If we trust God, we can show the world we, like Luke in the movie world and Job in our world, can win against all odds. By doing so we will prove to the Lord God that we really do love Him; and that nothing Satan does to us or our family will ever turn us against Him.

Jesus assures us our home will be secure when it is founded upon faith in him: "Therefore whosoever hears these sayings of mine, and does them, I will liken him unto a wise man, which built his house upon a rock: And the rain descended, and the floods came, and the winds blew, and beat upon that house; and it fell not: for it was founded upon a rock" (Matthew 7:24-25).

*"It is your destiny. Join me,
and together we can rule the galaxy."*
—Darth Vader

Chapter 5

THE HEAVYWEIGHT
BATTLE OF THE AGES

Star Wars is a story of battles. *Episode I* features fighting that skips from "the medieval to modern, from the doddering aristocracy of the Galactic Republic to the brutal opportunism of the Trade Federation, which has blocked all shipping routes to the planet Naboo," says *Time*. At the climax of the story in the final film, *The Return of the Jedi*, Luke Skywalker and Darth Vader climbed into the ring for a final bout that will determine the future of the universe. The Rebel Force faced defeat. Luke Skywalker, the number one power of the good Force, was the last hope. Darth Vader, the power of the dark Force, was the definite favorite.

In a real world fight that closely parallels this battle, Satan went to battle with Jesus Christ. The ambition of Satan knows no limit. First, he dared to try and overthrow the throne of God in Heaven. Then he tried to steal the affections of God's beloved creatures in Eden. He assaulted the family of Job, the great man of faith in his ancient times. Now he confidently crawls into the ring to battle Jesus Christ.

The timing of the fight is brilliant. Satan patiently waits thirty years, until the Son of God has fasted for forty days. His body is limp—his mind hardly able to function because of hunger. Satan never fights fair.

There is not the fanfare of a Las Vegas boxing match with all the advance advertisement, flashing spotlights, and screaming supporters. Jesus faced Satan in the wilderness all alone: "Then was Jesus led up of the Spirit into the wilderness to be tempted of the Devil" (Matthew 4:1).

The Devil is not impressed with his opponent's position as the Son of God. And we can be certain he is not impressed with our morals, church work, years of service, or godly parents. A confident Satan may wait years for us to reach our weakest moment, then he will give us the fight of our life.

In his fight plan for the battle with Jesus, Satan uses his three most powerful moves.

I. The dark Force offers pleasure to replace your pain

First is the appeal to pleasure. Luke's body, tired from his sword fight with Vader, is about ready to collapse. Darth Vader says, "You are beaten. It is useless to resist. Don't let yourself be destroyed." Vader is determined to get Luke to join the dark Force. The choice is clear. He could refuse and die. Or Luke could submit to Vader, relieve his tired body and enjoy all the luxury of the Empire.

Like Vadar, the Devil first opened his wilderness battle with a subtle appeal for pleasure. He suggests the gratifi-cation of eating. The Bible says, "And when he had fasted forty days and forty nights, he was afterward an hungered. And when the tempter came to him, he said, If you be the Son of God, command that these stones be made bread" (Matthew 4:2-3). After forty days without eating, this would be tempt-ing. The passion for food exploded within Jesus' body.

This appears as innocent as Eve taking a bite of fruit. What harm could there possibly be in turning a stone to bread and satisfying his body's cry for food? Hadn't God given him the appetite? Hadn't God provided opportunity for him to sat-isfy this appetite. Wouldn't it be very healthy to eat? Cer-tainly, this could in no way harm anyone else. Why not do it?

The answer to these questions is that it is never right to obey the Devil, no matter how much pleasure it would bring. "Know you not, that to who you yield yourselves ser-vants to obey, his servants you are to who you obey; whether of sin unto death, or of obedience unto righteousness?" (Ro-mans 6:16). If Luke had obeyed the dark Force, he would have become its servant. If Jesus had obeyed the Devil, he would have become the Devil's servant. No amount of pleas-ure is worth this.

The bizarre practices of witchcraft, Satanism, and voodoo are based on the premise of pleasure. Adolescent psy-chologist Michael Weiss said, "Satanism gives them the promise of power and privilege beyond anything they ever imagined. Not only can they have everything they want . . . but can do so while totally indulging themselves in drugs, sex, or any momentary pleasure."[10]

Anton Szandor LaVey, pastor of the First Church of Satan, declares the church is, "A temple of glorious indul-gence." His Satanic Bible says the nude woman that lays on the altar at their meetings serves as a "focal point towards

which all attention is focused during a ceremony." LaVey says she enables him to keep the audience's attention focused on the fulfillment of lust. That, he says, is what Satanism is all about.[11]

Satan is herding the masses with his constant call to "pleasure," "enjoyment," "excitement," and "self-indulgence" and "fun." Madison Avenue advertisements reinforce the idea that every desire deserves immediate fulfillment. It is not merely the times, or the culture, that is driving modern society, it is a headlong plunge into pleasure.

Abortion, teen pregnancy, and venereal disease are exploding as a result of Satan's call to sexual pleasure. His reasoning is that sex feels good and feeling good is what life is all about.

Little concern is given to damaging the ear drums, as thousands of young people flock to rock concerts. They are having fun. It feels good. That is all that matters.

Drug and alcohol indulgence cannot be checked because they satisfy the passion for pleasure. They enable people to escape the harsh realities of life by retreating into the fantasy land of intoxication.

No society in history has changed its values as drastically and suddenly as America did in the sixties. The changes that have rocked the foundation of the western world are all about pleasure. Without any shame, they have shouted their theme: "If it feels good do it."

The pleasure of fulfilling passion was what the dark Prince offered Jesus in the wilderness. It is what he is offering the masses of our wealthy, western world today. Evangelist Dave Breese said, "So the author of all evil, whose own heart is filled with violence, seduces legions to follow him. With neat finesse, he is often able to introduce drugs, illicit sex, and even violent crime as authentic moral symbols of that righteous rebellion...Only too much later does Satan's hapless victim realize, as he stands amid the wreckage of his life, that he has been duped by the Devil. He has been consumed by the fire that he started when he began to listen to the whispered suggestions of the evil one."[12]

"I didn't mean to let them take away my soul"

Linda Shaw kept finding signs that her 16-year-old son Derrick was involved in Satanism. He had filled his tenth grade school books with allusions to drugs, evil and death. In October of 1986, she confiscated his black candles, books of Satanic instruction, and a large hand-drawn pentagram. Finally, her son told her the truth, "Satan was his religion." What started out as fun and games, became a high, sensual pleasure and took control of his life.

Early on the evening of February 5, 1987 Derrick phoned Tara, a girl friend. He told her Satan had appeared in a blue light on the previous evening and demanded his soul. Derrick hung up the phone. He told his two younger brothers to keep their eyes closed. Derrick slipped down into the basement of the brick townhouse. He put a 30-30 rifle barrel into his mouth and pulled the trigger.

Derrick's mother placed the responsibility for her son's death on a two-year obsession with Satanism. The family's pastor placed the responsibility for that obsession on pleasure. Rev. Hedley Hopkins, of the United Baptist Church, said, "Young people who are bored are trying to make contact with evil. And if you try long enough, you eventually find something intelligent and malignant and destructive on the other end of the line."

In his last act before taking his life, Derrick wrote, on the back of a class schedule, "There must be some mistake, I didn't mean to let them take away my soul."[13] No one ever does. They merely want to follow the Devil's innocent suggestion to turn the stone to bread, to eat and enjoy the pleasure.

Jesus dodged His opponent's offer of pleasure and countered, "It is written, Man shall not live by bread alone, but by every word that proceedeth out of the mouth of God" (Matthew 4:4). This is the move that whips our adversary. The Word of God is the powerful weapon the Devil cannot withstand. Jesus merely quoted it. He does not reason with the Devil. He does not offer his opinions. He rapidly fires back with the Word of Scripture. This is a weapon every Christian can use. It is one that proved its effectiveness in the wilderness battle.

In reality, Satan could not care less about our pleasure. He is enticing us to death. For those seeking the ultimate, lasting pleasure Psalms 16:11 declares, "In your presence is fulness of joy." To know Him, to live in His presence; is heaven on earth. This is the ultimate pleasure and a person does not have to follow Satan's suggestions to find it.

II. The Force offers fame
to replace our insignificance

Vader made a second appeal to turn Luke. He offered glory and fame: "You do not yet realize your importance." Luke is tempted with importance—with fame. He could have had great popularity with all the thousands on the Dark Side. Just a surrender to the evil Force could have made him a glorious celebrity.

In the wilderness battle, Satan made a similar appeal to Jesus' pride: "Then the devil takes him up into the holy city, and set him on a pinnacle of the temple, And said unto him, If you be the Son of God, cast thyself down: for it is written, He shall give his angels charge concerning you: and in [their] hands they shall bear you up, lest at any time you dash your foot against a stone. Jesus said unto him, It is written again, You shall not tempt the Lord your God" (Matthew 4:5-7).

Satan said, "Show off. Jump. Every eye will be on you. You will be the talk of the town. Prove you are superior to all others. People will adore you. You will be famous. Your popularity will know no bounds."

The book, "*Satanism,*" by Schwarz & Duane Empey, says Satan "offers an intellectual challenge. In God, we are restricted and unable to choose a more pleasurable way. Satan worship, especially in its more intellectual forms, provided a chance to unlock the secrets of the universe, to step outside the mundane, the ordinary, the structured, into a world only a privileged few ever attain."[14]

"They want attention," was the reason one expert gave for the April, 1999 Colorado school massacre that killed 15. The two young killers committed suicide at the crime scene. They got world-wide fame, but it cost them everything. This shows how Satan can get some youth to sell their soul for a moments fame.

The appeal of pride is bringing widespread victories to the dark Force. It causes young people to become conceited and constantly criticize their classmates. Pride stubbornly refuses to consider the needs of other members of the family. It will never forgive wrongs. Pride will not say, "I'm sorry." It insists on having its own way. It overdresses to look superior. Pride buys more house and takes more vacation than a family can afford. It causes business men to buy more buildings and equipment than they need. Pride causes people to buy things on credit to impress others, which contributed to the 1.8 million Americans that went bankrupt in 1998.

The Bible says it plainly, "Pride goeth before destruction, and an haughty spirit before a fall. Better it is to be of an humble spirit with the lowly, than to divide the spoil with the proud" (Proverbs 16:18-19).

Little Richard, the rock-and-roll great, once told me how pride and ambition drive many musicians. He said many of the top rock musicians make pacts with Satan: "They will pray to the Devil and drink blood before a concert. They will say, 'Satan help me move this audience, help me be great and I will give you my soul'." If a person is willing to sell their soul for fame, the Devil is eager to deal with them.

The truth is you can be famous on earth, die, and no one ever heard of you. There will be great, lasting fame for those who reign in heaven with Jesus for all eternity.

III. The Force offers power to replace our frailty

In his final effort to get Luke to sell out, Darth Vader offered to give him the throne of the universe and all its powers. He urges, "It is your destiny. Join me, and together we can rule the galaxy." He can be the most famous figure in the universe. Planets will bow to him. All he has to do is turn to the dark side. It was a powerful appeal to Luke's pride, an offer hard to turn down.

Again, Darth Vader told Luke Skywalker, "You have only begun to discover your power." Luke resists, saying, "I'll never join you!" Vader tempted, "If you only knew the power of the dark side...The Emperor will show you the true nature of the Force."

As in *Star Wars*, Satan saved his most appealing offer to Jesus until last. "The devil takes him up into an exceeding high mountain, and shewed him all the kingdoms of the world, and the glory of them; And said unto him, All these things will I give you, if you wilt fall down and worship me" (Matthew 4:8-9). He said, "You can sit on the throne and rule this world. You can have power over its armies, its finances and its nations. Imagine the power this will give you. Why should you walk the dusty roads as a frail man in sandals when you can have the power of a world dictator?"

Many people have sold their soul to satisfy their passion for power. The athlete takes the illegal steroids to gain physical power. The business man gives a bribe to win a contract and gain economic power. The young woman surrenders her virtue to gain sexual power. The politician compromises his convictions to gain political power. Power tempts all the frail members of the human race.

Parents often have difficulty understanding why good kids are attracted by witchcraft and Devil worship. The reason is it has all the classic appeals that Satan made to Jesus. He offers them the pleasure of free drugs and group sex orgies. The Devil offers them fame and attention of the school group where everyone notices their black dress and adorning Satanic symbols. But the greatest appeal is that of power.

The Tempter won in Georgia

Terry Belcher, 16, told a Douglas County, Georgia jury he and a friend killed a 13-year-old girl to get "more power." Before his fourteenth birthday, Terry joined a secret Satanic cult. Later, he formed his own group in an abandoned house. There they regularly sacrificed dogs, cats and chickens to the Devil. Members of the cult drank the blood of the animals and ate their entrails and eyeballs. Those who refused were beaten. Terry said they held their ceremonies, "for power, a ritual, the taste of blood. I got money, power, sex, drugs, anything I wanted. It was easier to get 'em. It was like Satan helped you get 'em." The group listened to their favorite singer, Ozzy Osbourne sing "Bark at the Moon," from

Friday night until Sunday. Then a friend of Belcher slipped a leather bootlace around 13-year-old Teresa's neck. He pulled it tighter and tighter until it cut off her breath. She slumped to the floor dead. Then the group gathered around, and began chanting over her dead body, calling on Satan to appear.

In his murder trial, Terry was asked why they killed Teresa. He explained there was another group of Satanists in the area that was offering animal sacrifices. He said they wanted to offer Satan a human sacrifice so they would have "more power" than the rival group. Terry ended up sitting in a cell in Douglas County Prison, a picture of frailty. The Devil deluded him into believing his promise of power.[15]

Jesus countered the Devil's pitch for power with this bold declaration of the Word of God: "Then said Jesus unto him, Get you hence, Satan: for it is written, You shall worship the Lord your God, and him only shall you serve. Then the devil left him, and, behold, angels came and ministered unto him" (Matthew 4:10-11). Jesus won!

Cassandra met the victor

And Jesus is still winning—still the Champion. Cassandra Hoyer is proof. She used to be a high priestess of Satanism, living in terrible bondage. Today, through faith in Jesus Christ, she has been set free. The tall, attractive, former model, told church members of the horror that filled her life from the day her mother turned her over to the Satanists. She saw her twin sister, who was born with a deformed foot, ritually murdered. She said, "they put her on this little altar, and they chopped her head off." The girls were five at the time.

Cassandra became pregnant at 13. She was terrified at the thought of having some inhuman offspring. After her ritual rapes, dead cats or snakes were left between her legs. She was starved until she was willing to eat human flesh and drink blood and urine. They used drugs, hypnosis and separation from friends to brainwash her. At her lowest point she turned into an animal, clawing and eating plants and pages from the Bible.

At the age of 17 they released her and she entered a normal world for the first time. This did not end her trouble. When she helped police in their investigation of ritual murders, the cult members stripped her, spray-painted her body, and raped her at gun point. Cassandra said they called her a "Jesus brat." [16]

Cassandra says she overcame the Satanist's brainwashing and abuse through the power of Jesus Christ. She is living proof of Christ's victory over Satan.[17]

The young Christian marked this helpful verse in her pocket Bible, "Who shall separate us from the love of Christ? shall tribulation, or distress, or persecution, or famine, or nakedness, or peril or sword?...Nay, in all these things we are more than conquerors through him that loved us" (Romans 8:35-37).

Jesus won the victory over all of Satan's attacks and came out of the battle a winner. Through Him people like Cassandra can be delivered. Christ remains the heavyweight champion of the ages.

This deal is getting worse all the time.
—Lando

Chapter 6
THE GREAT BETRAYAL

Betrayals are brutal and not soon forgotten. Lando Calrissian, the great betrayer in the *Star Wars* story, is a most unusual person. He is a clone of the Ashandi family. His great-grandfather wanted many sons and cloned them from his own cells. Lando operated a gas mine he claims to have won in a "sabacca game."

When Han's space ship, the Millennium Falcon, developed serious engine trouble, he decided to go to Lando for help. Han assured Leia and his other passengers that Lando would treat them well because they were old friends.

As their ship came down on Lando's soft pink planet of Bespin, the clouds parted and the gleaming white metropolis came into sight. The Millennium Falcon landed on one of Cloud City's platforms. Lando led a large group out to meet

Han. He threws his arms around his long lost friend and embraced him. Lando led Han and Leia into a huge banquet room where they expect to eat. But when the mighty doors slide open, there at the far end of the table sat Darth Vader, who wanted to kill them. Lando tried to apologize for leading his friends into a trap: "I had no choice. They arrived right before you did. I'm sorry."

In a case like Lando's, Judas Iscariot betrayed Jesus for 30 pieces of silver. Here is the record: "Now the feast of unleavened bread drew nigh, which is called the Passover. And the chief priests and scribes sought how they might kill him; for they feared the people. Then entered Satan into Judas surnamed Iscariot, being of the number of the twelve. And he went his way, and communed with the chief priests and captains, how he might betray him unto them. And they were glad, and covenanted to give him money. And he promised, and sought opportunity to betray him unto them in the absence of the multitude" (Luke 22:1-6).

Why trust a suspicious man?

Han knew that Lando was a rascal. We have to wonder why he trusted him with his life and that of his friend? Likewise, Jesus knew what Judas was, and so we have to wonder why he picked him to be an Apostle? Jesus could see the Devil working and knew he was enticing Judas to betray him. Christ said, "But there are some of you that believe not.' For Jesus knew from the beginning who they were that believed not, and who should betray him" (John 6:64).

One reason Jesus picked Judas and made him the treasurer was to prove Christ's sincerity. The world had its spy in the camp and he was handling the money. When there is anything phony about a religion, it shows up in the money. But after Judas had betrayed Jesus, he declared, "I have sinned in that I have betrayed the innocent blood" (Matthew 27:4). A man who had watched Jesus and handled his money throughout his ministry said He was innocent—without any sin.

The Force's power to control

The Empire allowed Lando to prosper in return for his loyalty. He knew exactly who Princess Leia was and how intensely Vader wanted to kill her. But Lando deliberately betrayed his longtime friend Han and the hunted Princess into the hands of a murderer. It demonstrates what power the Emperor had over people.

Picking Judas also showed people how powerful the Devil is. Judas forever reminds us that the Devil can control unbelievers. The Devil entered Judas' body, took control, and used him to commit a horrible betrayal. He delivered the One who called him "friend" into the hands of those waiting to kill Him.

Judas had not been a perfect man, but for years he had been a good man, good enough that those who knew him best never suspected he was the betrayer. His fellow disciples who had lived and worked with him for three years suspected themselves more than Judas. When Christ declared "one of you will betray me," they walked out mumbling, "Is it I?" "And in the evening he comes with the twelve. And as they sat and did eat, Jesus said, Verily I say unto you, One of you which eats with me shall betray me. And they began to be sorrowful, and to say unto him one by one, Is it I? and another said, Is it I?" (Mark 14:17-19).

The Force's power to mislead

Judas should have understood the power of the Devil. He had been listening the day Jesus warned the upstanding, religious Pharisees about Satan's power. The Pharisees "Said unto him, Abraham is our father. Jesus said unto them, If you were Abraham's children, you would do the works of Abraham. But now you seek to kill me, a man that has told you the truth...You do the deeds of your father. Then said they to him, We be not born of fornication; we have one Father, even God. Jesus said unto them, If God were your Father, you would love me: for I proceeded forth and came from God....You are of your father the devil, and the lusts of your father you will do. He was a murderer from the beginning, and abode not in the truth, because there is no truth in him. When he speaks a lie, he speaks of his own: for he is a liar, and the father of it. And because I tell you the truth, you believe me not" (John 8:39-45).

Christ plainly warns that all men who have not been converted are the children of the Devil. They have the Devil's evil nature. They love sin and even when they realize its harm, they have no power to resist the Devil's commands. His lusts they will do. Satan lusted to see Jesus betrayed and crucified. Poor Judas did exactly what the Devil wanted. He allowed his body to be used to betray his God: "And while he yet spoke, lo, Judas, one of the twelve, came, and with him a great multitude with swords and staves, from the chief priests and elders of the people. Now he that betrayed him gave them a sign, saying, Whomsoever I shall kiss, that same is he: hold him fast. And forthwith he came to Jesus, and said, Hail, master; and kissed him. And Jesus said unto him, Friend, wherefore art you come? Then came they, and laid hands on Jesus, and took him" (Matthew 26:47-50).

So with a kiss, a show of affection, Judas betrays the Lord to the enemies who will crucify Him. This is how Lando betrayed Han, with a show of affection. He greeted him and hugged him as he led him into a trap.

Some try to deny Satan's power. They say Judas just did it for money. But he didn't keep the money. He took it back. Others say he was tired of following Christ and wanted to go home. But Judas didn't go home. He went out and hung himself. This man's downfall can only be explained by these words: "Then entered Satan into Judas surnamed Iscariot" (Luke 22:3).

The Force's power to entrap

The Empire tricked the traitor Lando. When he found they were going to give Han to a bounty hunter and that Leia and Wookiee would never leave the city alive, he realizes he has been fooled. Lando protested, "That was never a condition of our agreement." The terrifying Vader said, "Perhaps you think you're being treated unfairly." "No," a cowed Lando replied. After Vader leaves the room, Lando walked away muttering, "This deal is getting worse all the time." But, it was too late to back out.

Judas also realized he had made a bad deal when he saw what was happening: "When the morning was come, all the chief priests and elders of the people took counsel against Jesus to put him to death: And when they had bound him, they led him away, and delivered him to Pontius Pilate the governor. Then Judas, which had betrayed him, when he saw that he was condemned, repented himself, and brought again the thirty pieces of silver to the chief priests and elders, Saying, I have sinned in that I have betrayed the innocent blood. And they said, What is that to us? see you to that. And he cast down the pieces of silver in the temple, and departed, and went and hanged himself" (Matthew 27:1-5).

Judas had many reasons for thinking he was on the right road—the road to eternal life in heaven. Judas had made a profession of his faith when he walked the isles of humility following Jesus. He, like all the disciples, was baptized. Judas had not only witnessed Christ performing miracles, but had performed them himself: "And when he had called unto him his twelve disciples, he gave them power against unclean spirits, to cast them out, and to heal all manner of sickness and all manner of disease. Now the names of the twelve Apostles are these; The first, Simon, who is called Peter, and Andrew his brother; James the son of Zebedee, and John his brother; Philip, and Bartholomew; Thomas, and Matthew the publican; James the son of Alphaeus, and Lebbaeus, whose surname was Thaddaeus; Simon the Canaanite, and Judas Iscariot, who also betrayed him" (Matthew 10:1-4). Judas healed the sick and won souls from the clutches of demons. Surely, it would seem, this meant he was a Christian and on the right road. But though he delivered others, he was not delivered.

Judas knew all about Christianity. He was discipled by Jesus Christ for three years. He held the highest office in the church—Apostle. He had left his family, traveled tirelessly, and sacrificed far more than most. But he still wasn't a true believer!

Judas confessed his sin but he did not repent of it. He said, "I have sinned in that I have betrayed the innocent blood" (Matthew 27:4) and then hung himself. C. M. Ward, the outstanding radio minister, pointed out that there is a difference between Judas betraying Jesus and Peter denying Jesus, but not a big difference. But, Ward said, there is all the difference in the world between, "putting a handkerchief to your eyes and a rope to your neck." Peter wept over his sin, turned from it and went on following his Lord. Judas despaired, walked away and hung himself.

Lando, like Peter, repented of his awful betrayal , and devoted himself to the service of his friend Han and his cause to the end.

The Force's power to disgrace

Lando's betrayal will live on in the memories of his friends. He worked hard to make it up to them later. But the stain remained.

Judas' crime will live forever. Two centuries have come and gone since Judas' betrayal of Christ. But people still don't name their children Judas. They do not even name their dogs Judas.

The shame was unbearable for him. He gave the 30 pieces of silver back and hung himself. But even his money was dirty: When he saw they were going to kill Jesus he saw himself condemned. "And the chief priests took the silver pieces, and said, It is not lawful for to put them into the treasury, because it is the price of blood. And they took counsel, and bought with them the potter's field, to bury strangers in. Wherefore that field was called, The field of blood, unto this day. Then was fulfilled that which was spoken by Jeremy the prophet, saying, And they took the thirty pieces of silver, the price of him that was valued, who they of the children of Israel did value; And gave them for the potter's field, as the Lord appointed me" (Matthew 27:6-10).

But Judas did not bear the disgrace alone. His family had to suffer for the father's betrayal. Acts 1:25, a passage about finding a replacement for Judas, refers back to a prophetic Psalm which tells us Judas had a family: "Set you a wicked man over him: and let Satan stand at his right hand. When he shall be judged, let him be condemned: and let his prayer become sin. Let his days be few; and let another take his office. Let his children be fatherless, and his wife a widow. Let his children be continually vagabonds, and beg: let them seek their bread also out of their desolate places. Let the extortioner catch all that he has; and let the strangers spoil

his labor. Let there be none to extend mercy unto him: neither let there be any to favour his fatherless children. Let his posterity be cut off; and in the generation following let their name be blotted out. Let the iniquity of his fathers be remembered with the LORD; and let not the sin of his mother be blotted out" (Psalms 109:6-14). Judas' children were left fatherless vagabonds who begged bread and his wife a disgraced widow.

The Bible says after he died, Judas went "to his own place:" "Judas by transgression fell, that he might go to his own place" (Acts 1:25). Judas does not merely crawl into a grave and hide from his sins. He lived on beyond the grave in his own place. Man's soul is immortal.

And what is Judas' place? Is it heaven? Or, is it hell? Jesus leaves no room for doubt about Judas' eternal fate: "The Son of man indeed goes, as it is written of him: but woe to that man by whom the Son of man is betrayed! good were it for that man if he had never been born" (Mark 14:21). It would have been better if Judas never touched his mother's face, grown up, married, and brought children into the world. For after all this he betrayed Jesus and went to hell.

Judas had heard Jesus warning about losing his soul: "And fear not them which kill the body, but are not able to kill the soul: but rather fear him which is able to destroy both soul and body in hell" (Matthew 10:28). He heard this teaching, but he failed to heed. Now he is not merely hearing about hell, but Judas feels the searing pains from the fire and brimstone.

And so the evil Force's devastation of Judas will never end. His sullen moans and tortured groans will go on forever and forever. From eternity, Judas tells us we must do more than profess religion or hold positions in the church. We must genuinely believe Jesus for the power to overcome the dark Force.

Slowly, hesitantly, Luke removes the mask
from his father's face. There beneath the scars
is an elderly man. His eyes do not focus.
But the dying man smiles at the sight before him.

Chapter 7
THE SEVEN MASKS

Masks can hide the most horrible evil. And *Star Wars* is a story of masked people. Sometimes the masks served the purpose of sustaining life, as is the case of the oxygen masks. But at other times the masks served to hide the hideous dark Force.

Satan, the menace of the earth, hides behind masks that can even fool the careful observer. Mankind's enemy is threatening enough because of his power. But, when you add to his strength the ability to hide, he becomes an even more dangerous foe. The Devil's masks enable him to: "deceive the nations" (Revelation 20:8). Deception means…"to lead astray; to convince that truth is error and error is truth," or to convince men they're right when actually wrong." This diabolical deception knows no limits: "And the great dragon was cast out, that old serpent, called the Devil, and Satan, which deceives the whole world" (Revelation 12:9). Think of it; Satan has the ability to deceive "the whole world."

The Devil's obituary will read, "And the devil that deceived them was cast into the lake of fire and brimstone, where the beast and the false prophet are, and shall be tormented day and night for ever and ever" (Revelation 20:10). He will not be remembered for his power to seduce with sex, or to tempt with earth's treasures, but for his power to deceive.

The danger of deception

No one would obey the Devil if they recognized him. But the great Deceiver has demonstrated his ability to fool people by hiding behind masks. Knowing the destructive powers of deception, God warns us over and over about the danger of being deceived:

"Take heed that no man deceive you" (Matthew 24:4).

"Many shall come...and shall deceive many" (Matthew 24:5).

We are like naive little children, who are easily led astray: "Little children, let no man deceive you" (I John 3:7).

"And Jesus answering them began to say, Take heed lest any man deceive you" (Mark 13:5).

If God did not intervene, the Devil would deceive "the very elect" (Matthew 24:24).

The Deceiver can lead people to commit sins that bring God's anger down upon them: "Let no man deceive you with vain words: for because of these things comes the wrath of God upon the children of disobedience" (Ephesians 5:6).

No human is too intelligent to be deceived. Even the brilliant, educated, experienced Apostle Paul confessed he had been deceived: "For we ourselves also were sometimes foolish, disobedient, deceived, serving divers lusts and pleasures, living in malice and envy, hateful, and hating one another" (Titus 3:3).

Star Wars is a story of seven masks. Likewise, the Bible account of Satan is a story of seven masks.

1. The "beauty" mask

The evil Empire's deadly stormtroopers were clothed in dazzling white suits and beautiful snow-white masks. The prettiest of all the masks helped them hide in the snow and kill their unsuspecting prey.

Like the Empire's killers, Satan masks himself with great beauty. In Heaven his wicked ambitions were hidden behind a pretty covering that looked like diamonds and gold: "every precious stone was your covering" (Ezekiel 28:13). A large host of heavenly angels were deceived into following this evil rebel who looked so beautiful on the outside.

Satan fooled Adam and Eve by appearing as a beautiful serpent. The "serpent" was from creation "an angel of light." " Before being cursed to slither on the ground, the serpent was lovely. Eve was fooled by the creature's beautiful brightness. And so mankind was led from God into a world of suffering, pain and death.

Beauty is deceiving. A beautiful young woman can hide an evil heart and persuade a man to sell his soul.

A beautiful home can mask a terrible temptation and persuade a family to borrow their way into bankruptcy.

A beautiful cathedral can mask a false religion and persuade a soul to believe the lies being taught there.

Mankind is warned, "Be not deceived" because the very beautiful can contain the very bad. Demons are hidden by the loveliest masks.

2. The "friend" mask

Han's friend Lando Calrissian wore a mask that hid the face of the betrayer who will turn Han over to his enemies.

The Bible says the Deceiver hid within the bodies of Job's best friends to try and convince him God was causing his suffering and pain.

Joseph made friends with Pharaoh's butler while the two were in Egypt's prison. Joseph helped him by giving him the interpretation of a dream. In return, Joseph asked the butler, "Think on me when it shall be well with you, and shew kindness, I pray you,...and make mention of me unto Pharaoh, and bring me out of this house" (Genesis 40:14). But friends fail. After his release from prison, the butler forgot him: "Yet did not the chief butler remember Joseph, but forgot him" (Genesis 40:23).

King David was led astray by a friend and guide who worshipped with him: "For it was not an enemy that reproached me; then I could have borne it: neither was it he that hated me that did magnify himself against me; then I would have hid myself from him: But it was you, a man mine equal, my guide, and mine acquaintance. We took sweet counsel together, and walked unto the house of God in company" (Psalms 55:12-14).

The prophet Micah advised, "Trust you not in a friend" (Micah 7:5). Friends are wonderful assets, but it is possible to put too much trust in them. No friend is so foolish that he does not sometime give good advice and no friend is so wise that he does not sometime give bad advice. People must always remember that the dark Force can be hiding within a friend to misdirect them.

3. The "relations" mask

Wookies, the *Star Wars* wonder animals, wear masks.

These affectionate creatures are like giant pets, with a close relationship to the Rebels.

Satan deceives humans best when he hides within their close relations. Satan chose the wife of Job for a mask, to tell him his situation was hopeless and he should: "Curse God and die." He chose another close relationship when attacking Samson. It was the trusted Delilah, who would lead him to destruction: "And it came to pass afterward, that he loved a woman in the valley of Sorek, whose name was Delilah. And the lords of the Philistines came up unto her, and said unto her, Entice him, and see wherein his great strength lies, and by what means we may prevail against him, that we may bind him to afflict him: and we will give you every one of us eleven hundred pieces of silver" (Judges 16:4-5). Delilah sold out Samson to the Philistines, who gorged his eyes out and threw him in prison.

Delilah was evil. Job's wife was good. But, both served as masks for the Devil. The Force has the ability to use the words of those we love the most. This is why the Bible warns about putting too much trust in them: "Keep the doors of your mouth from her that lies in your bosom. For the son dishonoureth the father, the daughter riseth up against her mother, the daughter in law against her mother in law; a man's enemies are the men of his own house" (Micah 7:5-6).

While mates have the potential of being the greatest help we have in this world, and all relations can be of helpful support, there is a danger. Satan knows he often has no better place to hide than within someone we love. What better way to deceive a man than by using close relations to lead him astray?

4. The "mind" mask
Luke Skywalker wore a mask upon his face. He be-

came the strongest possessor of the good Force after Ben died in *A New Hope*. Yet his own mind was a mask hiding the fears and temptations of the dark Force.

Satan hides well when he hides within a person's mind. We are told to search our mind for any thoughts that are against God: "For the weapons of our warfare are not carnal, but mighty through God to the pulling down of strong holds; Casting down imaginations, and every high thing that exalteth itself against the knowledge of God, and bringing into captivity every thought to the obedience of Christ" (II Corinthians 10:4-5).

"It is as easy to deceive one's self without perceiving it, as it is difficult to deceive others without their finding it out," declared the French moralist Francois Rochefoucauld.

"Many an honest man," writes Christian Nestell Bovee an American author and editor. "practices on himself an amount of deceit, sufficient, if practiced on another, and in a little different way, to send him to the state prison."

Scripture declares, "If we say that we have no sin, we deceive ourselves" (I John 1:8). The unseen dark Force can permeate the mind of man and actually convince the wickedest person that they have not done anything wrong. How many humans are deceived by their own mind? The Bible says the majority of people fool themselves into thinking they are real good, when they aren't: "Most men will proclaim every one his own goodness: but a faithful man who can find?" (Proverbs 20:6).

Even after committing the most obvious of sins, the mind can convince a person they have done nothing wrong. The Bible says "an adulterous woman...wipeth her mouth, and said, I have done no wickedness" (Proverbs 30:20).

The mind of the worst hypocrite can convince them they are good people on their way to heaven: "Search the scriptures; for in them you think you have eternal life...And you will not come to me, that you might have life" (John 5:39-40).

5. The "angel" mask

Irvin Kershner, who worked on the *Star Wars* film *The Empire Strikes Back,* said that during the monstrous slug attack in the crater, "I wanted the actors to wear oxygen masks in this sequence, but I didn't want the masks to cover their faces entirely. So I had to make the masks really small."

Oxygen masks appear to be pumping life but they can also be hiding death. The Devil himself can appear as an angel: "Satan himself is transformed into an angel of light. Therefore it is no great thing if his ministers also be transformed as the ministers of righteousness; whose end shall be according to their works" (II Corinthians 11:14-15). Intelligent, observant humans can look the Devil in the eye and believe they are seeing an "angel of light!"

God advised us not to put too great a trust in His angels: "His angels he charged with folly" (Job 4:18). God was once betrayed by the angel Lucifer and his angelic followers when they rebelled against Him.

Angels are wonderful "ministering spirits," which help Christians. But a person has to check out angels by the Bible. Otherwise, he could follow a demon who just looks like an angel. Many false religions have been started by revelations from angels.

6. The "miracle" mask

The Tusken Raiders, or Sand People, who attacked Luke wore masks. Ralph McQuarrie, who helped create *Star Wars,* said, "George (Lucas) described the Tusken Raiders to me as nomads in the desert, Bedouin type of people. I could have created some alien-type creatures, but I simply decided to give them this mask instead. I knew they were going to have to live in dust storms, and I decided that they were aliens that required an adaptive sort of breathing device to make their life on Tatooine possible."[18] The Tusken Raiders' mask miraculously enabled the wearer to breath.

Satan's collection of masks includes miracles, which he uses to fool people who think everything supernatural is the work of God. Some people say, "This has to be of God; it is a miracle." They do not realize that Satan can also perform miracles. The Bible says he, "Deceives them that dwell on the earth by the means of those miracles which he had power to do" (Revelation 13:14). Again, the Word of God says, "they are the spirits of devils, working miracles" (Revelation 16:14).

Moses, Aaron and Egyptian magicians were involved in a story of miracles. It went like this: "And the LORD spoke unto Moses and unto Aaron, saying, When Pharaoh shall speak unto you, saying, Shew a miracle for you: then you shall say unto Aaron, Take your rod, and cast it before Pharaoh, and it shall become a serpent. And Moses and Aaron went in unto Pharaoh, and they did so as the LORD had commanded: and Aaron cast down his rod before Pharaoh, and before his servants, and it became a serpent. Then Pharaoh also called the wise men and the sorcerers: now the magicians of Egypt, they also did in like manner with their enchantments. For they cast down every man his rod, and they became serpents: but Aaron's rod swallowed up their rods" (Exodus 7:8-12).

This story teaches three important things about miracles: God can perform miracles, the Devil can perform miracles, and in the end God will destroy the works of the Devil.

Star Wars: A New Hope showed how the good miracle Force could overcome the evil power. Artoo, Threepio, Luke, and Ben drove their landspeeder into the spaceport at

Mos Eisley. They started through the streets with caution because this was an evil place. Several combat-hardened stormtroopers, stopped them and start questioning them about the droids. Ben knows they will be dead if they are found out, so he uses the good Force to control the troopers' minds.

> **TROOPER:** Let me see your identification.
> Ben replies in a very cool, commanding voice. Miraculously, the trooper begins repeating everything Ben says.
> **BEN:** You don't need to see his identification.
> **TROOPER:** We don't need to see his identification.
> **BEN:** These aren't the droids you're looking for.
> **TROOPER:** These aren't the droids we're looking for.
> **BEN:** He can go about his business.
> **TROOPER:** You can go about your business.
> **BEN:** *(to Luke)* Move along.
> **TROOPER:** Move along. Move along.

And so the Rebel's good Force overcomes the dark Force of the Empire.

7. The "messiah" mask

The mask seen most often in *Star Wars* was Darth Vader's. Laurent Bouzereau, the author of *Star Wars: The Annotated Screenplays*, said, "The awesome, seven-foot-tall Dark Lord of the Sith makes his way into the blinding light of the main passageway. This is Darth Vader, right hand of the Emperor. His face is obscured by his flowing black robes and grotesque breath mask, which stands out next to the fascist white-armored suits of the Imperial stormtroopers."[19] After

his death, Vader's body was laid on a funeral pyre, still wearing his black mask. A torch lights the logs beneath Vader's body and it is over.

Like the dark Darth Vader, Satan disguises himself well. Sometimes he even appears as a messiah. Jesus said, "For there shall arise false Christs, and false prophets, and shall shew great signs and wonders; insomuch that, if it were possible, they shall deceive the very elect" (Matthew 24:24). The Devil is parading a host of false Christ and false messiahs across the world's stage.

The world got a great lesson on the danger of masked Messiahs from a California cult. Holy Week, 1997, was marred by the discovery they had committed the largest mass suicide in American history. Thirty-nine members of the Heaven's Gate religious cult cooperated to neatly and methodically end their lives. Like the first family, Adam and Eve, they lost their lives in a bid to "become as gods." In the garden paradise of Rancho Santa Fe, 39 cult members also lost their lives following a "messiah" named Marshall Herff Applewhite in an effort to step up to a level above human and be as gods.

The conflict between life and death escalated where it began—in a garden paradise. In the Garden of Eden, Adam and Eve were seduced into death. In the Racho Santa Fe tropical garden paradise, the Heaven's Gate cult was seduced to die. "Nestled in the hills 30 miles north of San Diego, Rancho Santa Fe is a swank enclave sprinkled with polo fields, country clubs and multi-million-dollar estates. Such stellar personages as Victor Mature, Jenny Craig, and Patti Page lived in this small town.

On Wednesday, March 26, 1997, the Wednesday between Palm Sunday and Easter, Rio DiAngelo, accompanied by his employer, made a grisly discovery at the lavish home of the cult members, where he had once belonged. Rio, a former cult member, was alerted by two videotaped messages FedExed to him with instructions. Rio returned from the grim scene looking pale and visibly upset.

Later, the police went from room to room finding groups of bodies throughout the $1.6 million mansion the inhabitants had called "the Monastery." Each member had closely shorn hair, and was wearing a black hand-made shirt, loose black trousers, and black Nike shoes. They were lying peacefully on beds and cushions covered by purple triangular shrouds. "There were 21 women and 18 men, ranging in age from their 20's to a 72-year-old. Many were in their 40's," officials said. Most of the dead were white, with two blacks and one of Hispanic origin.

"They were, in the end, cyberspiritualists who made their living—and posted their dying—on the Internet. Their 'Heaven's Gate' Web site looms like an epitaph: 'Red Alert,' the message begins, 'Hale-Bopp Brings Closure to Heaven's Gate.' The 39 members...believed they were going to hitch a ride to a better life aboard a spaceship trailing the Hale-Bopp comet," reported the *Associated Press*. They had systematically planned their deaths for months, even years. And they took great care not to leave a mess behind as they carried out their plan, leaving their belongings packed neatly beside their bodies, and passports, driver's licenses, and other identification in their shirt pockets. These were people who were intelligent enough to make a lot of money on the Internet. But they still could not see through Satan's deception. They followed Marshall Herff Applewhite to the grave.

When the list of the deceased was finally revealed, it contained some surprising people: The daughter of a federal judge, the brother of a TV star, the son of a retired telephone company chief executive officer...a 72-year-old grandmother

from Iowa, a one-time paralegal student, a Colorado ranch-owner who had lost a state election by 20 votes and had a bit part in the movie *Butch Cassidy and The Sundance Kid,* an Ohio postal worker; an English teacher, and their leader a Presbyterian minister's son, along with the former university professor, Marshall Applewhite.

"In its documents, the group described a worldview on the furthest fringes of millennialism with disconnected elements of Christianity interpreted through a thick lens of science fiction. In essence, its teachings boiled down to a belief in exalted purpose for a few, combined with an exceptionally grim view of life on an Earth where evil was in control—a heady mixture of profound hope amidst utter isolation," revealed the *Associated Press* report.

Theirs was a structured existence. "Each member was given a partner of sorts and encouraged to travel always in a pair." There were no drugs, no alcohol, and no communication with family or friends. They believed in celibacy; seven of the men were castrated, following the example of Applewhite. Television viewing was limited; programs had to be pre-approved. X-Files, E.T. and Star Trek were on the approved list. Members had assigned seats for the programs.

So ended the tragedy of a group of bright, intelligent, hard-working people who followed a false messiah to their death. They were sincere people who followed a messiah they thought was from God. Actually he was a masked Devil.

*"Search your feelings, Father. You can't do this.
I feel the Conflict within you. Let go of your hate."
His dying father replied, "It is too late for me, Son."*
—Return of the Jedi

Chapter 8
THE PHANTOM'S PREY

There are three groups of people who fall easy prey to the dark Force. Each group is represented by a principal *Star Wars* character. In the present world, the same three groups are also found in the church listening to the Word of God. Little do they know that an unseen Phantom is there to prey upon them.

Jesus said Satan comes with the innocence of a little bird who pecks a seed. He is as quiet as the silent sun quietly drawing water from the earth and drying up the seed. The deadly menace works as unnoticed as the vine which moves steadily up a plant and chokes it to death. But in the end, this seemingly innocent, silent enemy is destroying people.

Jesus sought to show mankind how the evil Force is preying upon those within the church. He gave the simple, clear, ageless parable to unveil how the enemy is working:

"And when much people were gathered together, and were come to him out of every city, he spoke by a parable: A sower went out to sow his seed: and as he sowed, some fell by the way side; and it was trodden down, and the fowls of the air devoured it. And some fell upon a rock; and as soon as it was sprung up, it withered away, because it lacked moisture. And some fell among thorns; and the thorns sprang up with it, and choked it. And other fell on good ground, and sprang up, and bare fruit an hundredfold. And when he had said these things, he cried, He that hath ears to hear, let him hear. And his disciples asked him, saying, What might this parable be? And he said, Unto you it is given to know the mysteries of the kingdom of God: but to others in parables; that seeing they might not see, and hearing they might not understand. Now the parable is this: The seed is the word of God. Those by the way side are they that hear; then comes the devil, and taketh away the word out of their hearts, lest they should believe and be saved" They on the rock are they, which, when they hear, receive the word with joy; and these have no root, which for a while believe, and in time of temptation fall away. And that which fell among thorns are they, which, when they have heard, go forth, and are choked with cares and riches and pleasures of this life, and bring no fruit to perfection. But that on the good ground are they, which in an honest and good heart, having heard the word, keep it, and bringeth forrth fruit with patience" (Luke 8:4-15).

Jesus explained that the heart of man is like soil. The Word of God is like seed capable of producing the fruit of godliness, character, happiness and a triumphant, productive life. But the Devil is at work to stop the Word from effectively bearing fruit in human lives. The story describes the three groups of people Satan preys upon.

The put off

Darth Vader is *Star Wars'* sad procrastinator. He waited too late to turn from the dark Force. As a youth he had been raised to serve the good Force. But he turned. His life was spent in the service of the dark Force. When he was dying his son begs him to turn back to the good Force: "Search your feelings, Father. You can't do this. I feel the conflict within you. Let go of your hate." His dying father replies, "It is too late for me, Son." Vader said he has put it off until it is "too late."

Vader is a picture of the millions who were raised in church. They heard the Gospel. They like the idea of love, forgiveness, and everlasting life. But they hesitated to open their hearts and truly trust in Jesus Christ.

Jesus said they are like the hardened wayside: "A sower went out to sow his seed: and as he sowed, some fell by the way side; and it was trodden down, and the fowls of the air devoured it" (Luke 8:5). Christ explains: "Those by the way side are they that hear; then comes the devil, and takes away the word out of their hearts, lest they should believe and be saved" (Luke 8:12).

The "put offs" sometimes sit upon the church pews and listen. They think there is plenty of time to think about the matter before taking so drastic a step as believing—as turning from their way of life to follow Jesus in faith. So they put the

matter off. They see no danger because they do not see their enemy. While they delay to open their hearts, the Word they have heard rests upon their soul like a seed upon unopened earth.

They are hardly aware when the Devil comes and takes away the Word. It happens as quickly as a little bird snatches up a seed and flies away. They forget all they heard in the church—all about God and the Gospel. They hurry busily through their fruitless lives to the grave and a hopeless eternity. A little bird which seemed so innocent has taken away the life that might have been.

The Bible warns us against neglecting our opportunity: "Therefore we ought to give the more earnest heed to the things which we have heard, lest at any time we should let them slip. For if the word spoken by angels was steadfast, and every transgression and disobedience received a just recompense of reward; How shall we escape, if we neglect so great salvation; which at the first began to be spoken by the Lord, and was confirmed unto us by them that heard him" (Hebrews 2:1-3).

The Devil gives every reason for putting salvation off. He knows if he can keep them today, he may keep them forever.

The shallow believer

Lando Calrissian is the shallow believer in *Star Wars*. He hated the evil side. Han said: "But he has got no love for the Empire, I can tell you that." Lando served on the side of the good Force, yet the dashing young man turned and made a deal with the evil Emperor and sells his friends for a profit.

Like Lando, some church members are shallow believers. They sit in the church, hear the Word of God, and despise evil. They open up their hearts to it a little, but not all the way.

Christ said of them, "And some fell upon a rock; and as soon as it was sprung up, it withered away, because it lacked moisture" (Luke 8:6). Jesus explained these people in this manner: "They on the rock are they, which, when they hear, receive the word with joy; and these have no root, which for a while believe, and in time of temptation fall away"(Luke 8:13).

These are the people who are excited about Jesus. They respond to the Gospel with joy. They join the church, get baptized, and attend services. They have every appearance of being Christians. Their friends and minister rejoice that they are members. But there is a problem. Their faith is shallow. They have not fully surrendered the depths of their heart to the Lord. On the surface all seems well. But there is no depth, no roots to nourish their faith. Quietly, without a sound, the sun draws away the moisture. They wither and weaken. Then the Devil makes his move. Temptation comes: there is a shady business deal, a stimulating sexual opportunity, a friend's invitation to a wild party. They go for it. This is the turning point. They fall away.

The worldly

Han Solo, the tough, roguish starpilot, represents the worldly. He introduces himself to Ben who is seeking a fast ship to war against the dark Force. Han says:" I'm captain of the Millennium Falcon. Chewie here tells me you're looking for passage to the Alderaan system." Ben replies, "Yes, indeed. If it's a fast ship." Han tells Ben, "It's going to cost you something extra. Ten thousand, all in advance." To get Han to be the pilot ends up costing Ben seventeen thousand. The man believes he is on the good side but he is extremely worldly. Money is everything.

Han Solo is a picture of the third group in the church Satan preys on— the worldly. They are the people who not only join the church, but through the years they seem to be maturing into fine Christians. They have some room in their heart for the Word of God. But other seeds are also growing. The seeds of worldliness are springing up beside the good plant. Slowly, ever so slowly, they creep up around it.

Jesus said, "And some fell among thorns; and the thorns sprang up with it, and choked it" (Luke 8:7). The Lord explained this portion of His parable in these words: "And that which fell among thorns are they, which, when they have heard, go forth, and are choked with cares and riches and pleasures of this life, and bring no fruit to perfection" (Luke 8:14).

These are the people in church who get off to a great start in their faith. They grow. Everyone about them can see the growth. There is great expectation for them. It appears certain that they will produce a lot of fruit. People begin to wonder if they will develop into Christian teachers, or preachers, or perhaps even missionaries. The signs are there.

But while the Word of God grows, the cares of this life, the desire for pleasure, and the love of this world are also growing. It is so slow that it is hardly noticed. The vines of this world gradually entangle the plant of the next world. Before the fruit can be produced, the life is taken from them. They are choked to death by the Devil. Slowly and tortuously the life that looked so good dies.

The Bible warns about such falling away: "For if after they have escaped the pollutions of the world through the knowledge of the Lord and Saviour Jesus Christ, they are again entangled therein, and overcome, the latter end is worse with them than the beginning. For it had been better for them not to have known the way of righteousness, than, after they have known it, to turn from the holy commandment delivered unto them. But it is happened unto them according to the true proverb, The dog is turned to his own vomit again; and the sow that was washed to her wallowing in the mire" (II Peter 2:20-22).

The true believers

Luke Skywalker is *Star Wars'* true believer. He starts out with a little faith in the good Force. Through studying, working, and fighting the dark Force, Luke grows into the strongest man among the Rebels.

Luke is an example of those in the church who will never be the evil Phantom's prey. Christ said, "And other fell on good ground, and sprang up, and bare fruit an hundredfold. And when he had said these things, he cried, He that has ears to hear, let him hear" (Luke 8:8). Jesus explained these people in this manner: "But that on the good ground are they, which in an honest and good heart, having heard the word, keep it, and bring forth fruit with patience" (Luke 8:15).

These are the Christians who have a good heart. They are the "good soil." Their lives keep on bearing fruit. Certainly not all Christians are the same. Some bear more fruit than others. But two things distinguish the genuine Christians, they bear fruit only God can produce and those that fell on good ground last. They do not fall away.

Taking back the dark Force's ground

I met a man in Haiti whose heart was good soil for the Word of God to produce good fruit. Despite all the Devil's efforts to stop him, he remained true. Ed Shreve spent his life as a missionary at Bay De Heine, Haiti. He was told by an older man of God, "Son, if you stay here you will need these words." He recited them to the young missionary who did not seem too interested. Ed ordered a river dammed up to save water for the crops and alleviate the starving. The natives informed him the witch doctors had put a curse on him for going in the water. He developed a choking sensation. Breathing became difficult. When Ed went to the doctors they could not find the trouble.

Finally, one night Ed could not fight it any longer. He was too exhausted to keep breathing. He began to lose consciousness. Everything went black. Ed said he felt he was falling down, down into darkness. He was sure he was dying. Suddenly, the words of the old missionary came before him, "Oh Satan, I take back all the ground that I have yielded to you consciously and unconsciously. I put between me and you the blood of the Lord Jesus Christ and dedicate my life anew to him." His breathing returned. His life returned, then he heard a pig squealing and running into the fence by his house. The next morning his wife came in and found him much better. She asked how he was and Ed replied, "I feel fine." Mrs. Shreve went outside and returned to inform him there was a dead pig by the fence. Ed remembered Gadara and how Jesus cast the evil spirits out of a man into the swine. They drove the herd off the cliff to their death. Shreve fully recovered and labored victoriously for over thirty years in the land of voodoo.

I was with Ed one December. He and his wife were teaching 2,000 children in their school. When I went home for the holidays, he and his wife spent Christmas distributing shoes to all the school children. For many, that would be the only pair they would have for the year. Thanks to Ed and his wife, thousands of children learned to read and write. And they learned about Jesus and victory over the Devil. Ed Shreve and his wife bore fruit faithfully throughout their entire lives.

We, like Ed, are in a war. This war rages between the power of Satan and the power of God. The Devil cannot stand it when we take our place with authority at the Cross. Here all the power of his curses are overcome. Decide now not to live another moment in fear or defeat. Boldly declare these words with Ed Shreve, "Oh Satan, I take back all the ground I have yielded to you consciously and unconsciously. I put between me and you the blood of the Lord Jesus Christ and dedicate my life anew to him."

Darth Vader taunts Ben as they fight,
"Your powers are weak, old man...You should not
have come back." No one understands Ben has to
die to get the plans for victory and to become a
spirit to guide them to that victory.
—Star Wars: A New Hope

Chapter 9
THE SECRET STEALTH ATTACK

Lies, like stealth planes, are very hard to recognize and extremely dangerous. In *Star Wars,* well disguised lies are essential to the story. The Emperor lies to Darth Vader. Han lies to Luke Skywalker, Lando lies to the Rebels, and even the good instructor Yoda lied to Luke. Those who win must recognize the lies and not heed them. If they trust the wrong words, they can die.

Likewise, the Devil has launched a secret stealth attack in the present world. The assault is spearheaded by some cunning and ruinous lies. Humans, on their journey through this universe, look for directions, for knowledge of what is right and what is wrong. They trust their minister, their reasoning, and their conscience. If these sources are not telling

the truth they will make wrong choices—choices that can destroy their life, family, and immortal soul.

The dark Force sought to demolish men by using the powerful weapon of lying. Jesus confronted the religious elite about their lies, "you are of your father the devil, and the lusts of your father you will do. He...abode not in the truth, because there is no truth in him. When he speaks a lie, he speaks of his own: for he is a liar, and the father of it" (John 8:44).

If just one small lie is told regarding the spacecraft at Mission Control in Cape Kennedy, the ship can be doomed and the astronauts destroyed. This catastrophe can be produced by just a few words from a trusted co-worker which are not truthful.

In the battlefield of the mind, the war rages between truth and error—between the true Words of God and the dishonest words of the Devil. The only survivors in the universe will be those who recognize the truth.

In the Old Testament Jewish world there was, "a lying spirit in the mouth...(of) prophets" (I Kings 22:23), enticing the people to their destruction.

In the New Testament times lying Apostles led people down the wrong path: "You have tried them which say they are Apostles, and are not, and have found them liars" (Revelation 2:2).

The book, *Satan's Evangelistic Strategy For This New Age* says the church is in danger of conceding the world to a Satanic religion of lies: "The New Age Movement has rushed in to fill the vacuum left by a timid and sometimes fearful church. May God keep us from the unbelief that would concede this world to Satan!"[20]

The Devil knows that what humans believe determines what they do, their character, and their eternal destiny. So, the dark Liar sometimes creeps inside religious men, puts on ministerial robes, climbs into pulpits, and presents deadly falsehoods. People listen to them and believe they are hearing the Word of God. As strange as is seems, Satan actually writes doctrines for churches: "Now the Spirit speaks expressly, that in the latter times some shall depart from the faith, giving heed to seducing spirits, and doctrines of devils; Speaking lies in hypocrisy; having their conscience seared with a hot iron" (I Timothy 4:1-2).

Four deadly lies are told in *Star Wars* and repeated in our world by Satan.

1. "Never trust the good Force"

Ben, the strongest power of the good Force, tells Luke his destiny lies in saving the galaxy from the evil Empire: "They must be delivered safely or other star systems will suffer the same fate as Alderaan. Your destiny lies along a different path...The Force will be with you...always!"

But Darth Vader says that is a lie of the good Force: "Your destiny lies with me, Skywalker. Obi-Wan knew this to be true." Luke recognizes the evil lie about his destiny calling for him to join the dark Force. He cried, "No!"

The fallen angel Lucifer told Eve the same lie. He declared God's words were not true: "And the woman said unto the serpent, We may eat of the fruit of the trees of the garden: But of the fruit of the tree which is in the midst of the garden, God has said, You shall not eat of it, neither shall you touch it, lest you die. And the serpent said unto the woman, You shall not surely die" (Genesis 3:2-4). The Devil's lie implied, "God could not be trusted; His words were false."

Puritan preacher Thomas Watson said the lie that God's word is not true is corrupting many lives: "This is Satan's masterpiece, if he can keep them from the belief of the truth, he is sure to keep them from the practice of it" This is why Satan fights the Word.

Dr. George Wald, a former professor of Biology at Harvard, showed just how important it is that we not embrace Satan's lie about God's Word. He received huge applause from the scholarly scientists gathered at Southern Colorado State College when he declared, "The only way the world is going to stop short of the brink of nuclear holocaust is a return to God and the principles of the Bible." Wald said the greatest question facing civilization today is this, "Is the Bible a revelation of the God who created the universe showing us the way out of our dilemma or is the Bible only an archaic book of folk stories written by men?" Here Dr. Wald clearly identified the real issue: "Is God's word a lie, or is it the truth?" This demonic lie about God's Word is being promoted by the popular book *A Course in Miracles*. Dean Halverson, formerly a researcher for the Spiritual Counterfeits Project, points out the course teaches God did not create the world, Jesus is not the only Son of God, and Christ did not suffer and die for our sins. According to the course, some "parts of the Bible have the Holy Spirit as their source. Other parts are from the ego."[21]

Popular New Age author David Spangler is spreading Satan's lie about God's Word. He writes, "We can take all the scriptures and all the teachings, and all the tablets, and all the laws, and all the marshmallows and have a jolly good bonfire and marshmallow roast, because that's all they are worth. Once you are the law, once you are the truth, you do not need it externally represented for you."[22]

This lie has echoed from Eden through the ages in the halls of learning, the sanctuaries of skeptics and even the church's seminaries. But the lie that we can't trust God's Word raises some interesting questions:

- If God's Word is a lie, how could it tell us the world was round in 740 B.C.? "He (God) sitteth on the circle of the earth" (Isaiah 40:22), when men of science declared it was flat?

- If God's Word is not true, explain how it taught us to quarantine sick people hundreds of years before man discovered contagious diseases? "All the days wherein the plague shall be in him he shall be defiled; he is unclean: he shall dwell alone; without the camp shall his habitation be" (Leviticus 13:46).

- How did the Bible teach hygiene 4,000 years ago in 160 passages, when no other ancient book did? Germs had not been discovered? "And when he that hath an issue is cleansed of his issue; then he shall number to himself seven days for his cleansing, and wash his clothes, and bathe his flesh in running water, and shall be clean" (Leviticus 15:13).

- If God's Word is not dependable, how did it record in 2,000 B.C. that there was nothing holding up the world? "He...hangs the earth upon nothing" (Job 26:7), when learned men said Hercules, a giant turtle, or strong pillars were its foundation. Only in 475 A. D. did Copernicus teach us better?

- If the Bible is not true how can doubters explain that it said in 600 B.C., "the host of heaven cannot be numbered," when scientists Hipparchus said in 725 A.D. that there were 1022 stars, and Ptolemy said in 200 A.D. there were 1026 stars? Finally Galileo said the stars could not be counted.

- If the Word of God is a lie, how did the following prediction come to pass? "Therefore say unto the house of Israel, Thus says the Lord GOD; I will take you from among the heathen, and gather you out of all countries, and will bring you into your own land" (Ezekiel 36:22,24). On May 14, 1948, the Jewish flag went up for the first time in 2,500 years and the Jews returned home. The writings of Buddha, Confucius, and Lao-tse contain no prophecy—no predictions of the future. Dr. James Kennedy says, "In the Koran (the writings of Muhammad) there is one instance of a specific prophecy—a self-fulfilling prophecy that he, Muhammad himself, would return to Mecca. This hardly equals Jesus' prophecy that He would return from the grave." Yet, a billion people now believe the Quran is the truth and the Bible is untrue.

Adam and Eve believed the lie that God's Word could not be trusted when it said they'd die if they ate the fruit. They ate it and they died. The Devil, not God, is the liar.

2. "You can become a god"

Darth Vader tried to turn Luke Skywalker to the dark side by promising him he could be the supreme ruler. "Luke. You can destroy the Emperor. He has foreseen this." The Emperor is the Supreme Ruler of the Galactic Empire and Master of the dark side of the Force. Everyone kneels to worship the Emperor, even Vader. If Luke became Emperor he would rule the universe. He would be the god.

The Devil's second seductive lie was that Adam and Eve could become gods: "For God doth know that in the day you eat thereof, then your eyes shall be opened, and you shall be as gods, knowing good and evil" (Genesis 3:5).

Ambitious people are tempted by the offer to become gods. Throughout history religious cults have enslaved people with this promise. California's Heaven Gate cult promised to carry men on a spaceship to the heights of heaven where they would be as gods. Utah's Joseph Smith promised that his followers would become gods and rule over their own planet after this life. Shirley MacLaine closed her TV drama, *Out on a Limb,* standing on a beach with arms reaching upward, declaring, "I am god. I am god."

Randall Baer said, "Humanism assigns man to a throne that spans the heavens and the earth in a divine heritage of universal lordship, omnipotence, and self-created glory." [23]

The Church of Satan recites a religious song from an occult tract called "The Emerald Book of Truth" and H.G. Wells' *The Island of Dr. Moreau.* The song included chants of:

> We are men. (Repeated)
> Man is God. (Repeated)

The Bible asks men who think themselves gods some interesting questions:

- Can you speak to the clouds and make it rain? "Can you lift up your voice to the clouds, that abundance of waters may cover you" (Job 38:34).
- Can you count the clouds? "Who can number the clouds in wisdom?" (Job 38:37).

- Can you stop the rain? "Or who can stay the bottles of heaven" (Job 38:37).
- Can you make lightening light the sky? "Can you send lightnings" (Job 38:35).

3. "You will not die"

The evil Emperor talks to Vader about living and reigning over the Empire. But while he calls Vader "friend," he really wants him dead. When Luke puts his sword against Vader's throat during a fight, the Emperor shows a pleasant reaction and cries, "Good" to Luke. Though he promised him he would live, it was all a lie.

Satan is as deceptive as the *Star Wars* Emperor. He talks to men about reigning as gods while he prepares their death. In Genesis 2:17, God told Adam and Eve, "But of the tree of the knowledge of good and evil, you shall not eat of it: for in the day that you eatest thereof you shall surely die." Satan contradicted this, saying, "You shall not surely die." But they did.

Today the Devil has convinced many people that they "shall not die." For example the New Agers do not believe anyone has ever died. "Death itself is an illusion," explains historian Christopher Lasch.[24]

One New Ager said "I am a firm believer in reincarnation. After all, if we're supposed to recycle, why shouldn't God? You only go around 60 million times—so grab the gusto." Thirty million Americans agree with his belief in reincarnation. [25]

4. "A sacrifice is not necessary"

The biggest lie of all is that Luke and Ben do not have to go into the Death Star where Ben will die. Luke's well meaning Uncle Owen said, "I told you to forget it." He tells

Luke he must stay on the farm and work. But Luke and Ben go to the giant Death Star to get the plans that will save the universe from the Emperor's destruction. Aboard the ship, Darth Vader taunts Ben as they fight, "Your powers are weak, old man...You should not have come back." No one understands Ben had to die to get the plans for victory and to become a spirit to guide them to that victory. Ben had to die for all the good Rebels to live.

The Devil's biggest lie was spoken by the Apostle Peter: "From that time forth began Jesus to show unto his disciples, how that he must go unto Jerusalem, and suffer many things of the elders and chief priests and scribes, and be killed, and be raised again the third day. Then Peter took him, and began to rebuke him, saying, Be it far from you, Lord: this shall not be unto you. But he turned, and said unto Peter, Get you behind me, Satan: you art an offense unto me: for you savour not the things that be of God, but those that be of men" (Matthew 16:21-23).

The Devil failed to entice Christ in the wilderness. Now he tries again through the lying words of a disciple. Peter was speaking a lie of the Devil. As they told Luke and Ben it was not necessary to go into Death Star where death awaits, Peter told Jesus it is not necessary for him to go into Jerusalem and die. Jesus responded by calling the great Apostle Peter, "Satan." It was absolutely essential that Christ die, otherwise, there would be no hope of winning over evil and no way for Jesus' Spirit to guide them to victory.

Today the lie from Peter's lips echoes throughout the world. It says the Cross is not necessary. You can do good works and save your self. But only the sinless blood of Jesus can cleanse men from sin. Only that blood can enable us to enter into God's heaven. Christ said, "This is my blood... which is shed...for many for the remission of sins." (Matthew

26:28).

Author Dave Breese writes, "The enemy has produced a significant triumph when he can spread in our society a broad set of false views about God, Christ, the Holy Spirit, sin, the purpose of life, and other imperative points of Christian doctrine. For every one person who is subverted by Satan worship, thousands are enmeshed in Satan's more deadly trap: doctrinal error....The witches and the magicians provide Satan with some fun and games along the way, but his real activity is subverting the insiders, the reasonable, and the semi-studious with false doctrine."[26]

Examples of the Devil's lie can be found in the most popular religions. The Hindu religion teaches that we are saved by working faithfully at ceremonies, duties and religious rites. Muslims are only guaranteed eternal bliss if they die fighting and killing the enemies of Allah. Muhammad said he was not sure he had done enough to make heaven. He said it all depended on what kind of mood Allah was in the day he died.

The Buddhist religion teaches that man is saved to a better earthly life through an endless cycle of births, deaths, and reincarnations to enter a better life by obeying five precepts: Eating no living thing, not stealing, not committing adultery, telling no lies, and not using drugs or alcohol.

But Christianity declares, "For by grace are you saved through faith; and that not of yourselves: it is the gift of God: Not of works, lest any man should boast" (Ephesians 2:8-9). The Christian motivation for living right is love. God loves man enough to freely give him eternal life through the cross. In appreciation, those who accept the gift seek to please him.

Ricky Kasso bought the lie

The power of Satan's lies can be seen in the case of

Gary Lawners. Gary was just another curly-headed teenager dabbling in the dark shadows of Satanism until the night of Thursday, July 5, 1984. That evening he was chosen to be the Devil's sacrifice. David St. Clair documented in his book, *Say You Love Satan*, that Ricky Kasso lifted a sacrificial dagger over Gary and shouted "Say you love Satan" "No. I love my mother," Gary answered. Ricky plunged the dagger into Gary's chest. A third youth, Jimmy Traiano, asked Ricky what he was doing. Ricky responded, "He has got to say he loves Satan."

Seventeen times the long, sharp blade tore into the body of Gary Lawners, one time right through his eye. As heavy metal music blared Ricky Kasso finished his sacrifice. Gary repeated his final words as he bled to death on a Satanic altar: "I love my mother."

Months later they found the Northport, Long Island youth's mutilated body. Detective Lieutenant Robert Dunn, commander of the Suffolk County Homicide Squad said: "This was a sacrificial killing. It's pure Satanism."

The whole episode began years before. Ricky Kasso got bored during the summer vacation. He wandered into a library and browsed through a section of books on the occult. Anton LaVey's *Satanic Bible* caught his attention. About that time the librarian said, "I am sorry but it is closing time." The next morning he was waiting when the local bookstore opened. As he bought a copy of LaVey's book, the clerk told him "that's powerful stuff."

After reading the *Satanic Bible*, Ricky concluded, "if this guy knows what he is talking about, Satan is the way to go." Ricky reasoned Jesus Christ was not interested in rock music. He was not there to boast you in your chemical highs. In the big decision of his short life, Ricky was convinced of a lie—that Satan was the way to go.

After they found Gary's body, Ricky was arrested and charged with murder. At 12:30 a.m., when the jailer did his bed check, Ricky appeared to be asleep on his cot. At 1:00 a. m. they found Ricky hanging from the cell door. He was dead.

The Rolling Stones found something of entertainment value in this bloody episode. They sang,

> "Hey Ricky, you're so fine,
>   Why doncha stab me one more time?
> Hey Ricky, you're a nice guy,
>   He stabbed me in the eye?
> Hey Ricky, you're so swell,
>   Why you hangin in your cell?"

"Ricky Kasso, Jimmy Troiano, and Gary Lawners were three boys from good homes," writes David St. Clair, in his book *Say you Love Satan*. "But by the time they reached high school they were cutting class, smoking marijuana, and doing heavier dope. Their classmates knew they were headed for trouble. No one dreamed they were into Satanism. Then one dark night in the chic town of Northport, Satan said to kill. Northport closed its eyes...high schoolers made the murder their unspoken secret and three boys were touched by violence and death."

Rickie Kasso bought the Devil's lie. He decided to trust Satan instead of the Bible. Satan's secret stealth attack cost him his friends, his future, his life and his all.

Do not...Do not underestimate
the powers of the Emperor
or suffer your father's fate you will.
—Yoda to Luke

Chapter 10

THE GREAT SEDUCER

Anakin Skywalker and Luke Skywalker started out alike. Both were very innocent children. Anakin and Luke would both aspired to be Jedis. Both trained hard and studied to reach their goals. Anakin became Vader, who will go down in history as one of the great evil figures. Luke became the great hero of the universe. Between the wicked loser Darth Vader and the heroic winner Luke Skywalker, there was but one difference— how they handled temptation. They give us a key *Star Wars* lesson that is essential to winning over the temptations of the dark Force.

Yoda, the great teacher of the Force told Luke, "Do not...Do not underestimate the powers of the Emperor or suffer your father's fate you will. Luke, when gone am I . . . the last of the Jedi will you be. Luke, the Force runs strong in your family. Pass on what you have learned, Luke . . ." and then Yoda catches his last breath and dies.

Yoda, the Master of the Force, left us a warning. We must not underestimate the powers of the evil Emperor. There is no person so wise, or strong, that he cannot be brought down by evil temptations. The Christian Apostle Paul expressed this concern about his fellow Christians in Thessolonica: "I sent to know your faith, lest by some means the tempter have tempted you, and our labor be in vain" (I Thessalonians 3:5).

The Tempter is extremely successful because people underestimate his power and are easily overcome by his temptations. While they see others falter and fall, they will not admit the Tempter could ever bring them down. Instead of admitting they are facing a supernatural enemy and need God's protection, these people merely explain away the fall of others.

- A kid goes wild and robs a store and they say, "Adolescence is a difficult time and they weren't well adjusted."

- Youth blow their minds away on drugs and people say, "They come from a dysfunctional home."

- Thirty-year-olds spend their way into bankruptcy and walk away leaving their babies to be raised by the grandparents. Friends comment, "They just weren't ready for marriage. They were just kids who hadn't learn to manage."

- A student runs into a school and kills his classmates. Community leaders say, "He was a loner who never learned to relate."

These people come up with little labels for evil acts because they do not want to admit the dark Tempter exists. They want to feel self-sufficient and secure. English author Francis Quarles warned, "The way to be safe is to never be secure." As long as we ignore Yoda's warning, "Do not....Do not underestimate the powers of the Emperor," we will be easy prey for the dark Force.

The seduced

The boy wants to drive and drive fast. Nothing else matters: the fact that he has been drinking, the lack of a reason to get there quickly, the chance of a traffic ticket and hundreds of dollars in increased insurance, nor the possibility of a wreck that may injure, maim, or kill. Later he will regret it. But though he doesn't understand why, he must push the accelerator and race down the highway, faster and faster, whatever the consequences.

The young girl wants to date a wild boy. Nothing else matters: the fact that he uses drugs and drinks, the lie she must tell her parents, the reputation she will lose at school, what her children will hear in years ahead, nor the embarrassment she may suffer. She has a passionate desire that makes no sense to parents or friends. Later she will regret it. But though she does not understand the reason why, she must have this date, whatever the consequences.

See, the man looks at an attractive woman and he wants her. Nothing else matters: his marriage, the woman's husband and children, pregnancy, infectious diseases, guilt, nor shame. There is a passionate desire for her that makes no sense to those who watch. Later it will make no sense to him. But though he does not understand the reason why, he must have her, whatever the consequences.

The woman wants to buy the coat. Nothing else matters: the fact that she does not have the money, the thousands she already owes on credit cards, the fact that she already has a perfectly good coat, the children's need for a college education, not the quarrels that may erupt. She has a passionate desire that makes no sense to a bookkeeper. Later she will regret it. But though she does not understand the reason why, she must buy the coat now, whatever the consequences.

These people are under a direct supernatural attack. They are being seduced by the dark Force. Their conduct makes no sense at all. Why they behave as they do defies all reason. The Bible calls their actions a mystery: "the mystery of iniquity doth already work...whose coming is after the working of Satan with all power and signs and lying wonders, And with all deceivableness of unrighteousness in them that perish" (II Thessalonians 2:7-10). Their conduct cannot be understood apart from a mysterious Tempter enticing and seducing them.

Star Wars not only gives a warning about the power of evil, but the film also shows us how to overcome the temptations of the dark Force. The film series contains seven lessons on winning over the Tempter.

Hold a good set of values

Luke overcame this Tempter with an unwavering set of values. When the Emperor used the threat of death to turn Luke he said, "You're gravely mistaken. You won't convert me." When he was offered a chance to turn to the dark Force and rule the universe, Luke said, "I will not turn...and you'll be forced to kill me."

He had a set of values that did not vary for anything. They were more important to Luke than wealth, power, and life itself. When we set our values by the standards of the Bible, we have taken the first step in defeating The Tempter.

England's great minister, Charles Hadden Spurgeon, made an interesting comment about education. He said, "Learn to say 'No;' it will be of more use to you than to be able to read Latin." Luke Skywalker learned to say no. It appeared the Emperor was about to kill Luke. He glances at his lightsaber, touching it he says, "You want this, don't you? The hate is swelling in you now. Take your Jedi weapon. Use it. I am unarmed. Strike me down with it. Give in to your anger. With each passing moment you make yourself more my servant." Luke cries back in agony, "No!"

Learn from others mistakes

Luke saw what the dark Force had done to his father, Darth Vader and to the Emperor. He learned from their mistakes. He did not give temptation a try and end up enslaved by it, like Vader did.

The lesson for us to learn is we do not have to try evil to learn what it is like. A Haight-Ashbury drug user told me, "Don't knock it if you haven't tried it." But this is nonsense. We don't have to rob a bank or kill someone to decide whether they are right or wrong. We can learn from the experiences of others. There are a lot of good obstetricians that never had a baby, but they do a good job of delivering one.

There is danger in trying evil, even once. As Yoda told Luke: "Once you start down the dark path, forever will it dominate your destiny." Jesus put this clearly, "I say unto you, Whosoever commits sin is the servant of sin" (John 8:34). Once we start yielding to temptation it is hard to turn back. By learning from others we can avoid the danger of trying sin for ourselves and ending up its slave.

Avoid instant gratification

Luke stayed focused on his long range goal of defeating the Empire and setting his people free. The tempter could not distract him with thoughts of what would feel good at the moment. *Star Wars* presents an interesting contrast to Luke in Jabba, a creature of instant gratification. *In the Return of the Jedi* we find him in his throne room with a beautiful dancer chained by his side. He is surrounded by a mob of degenerates. Han and Leia are his prisoners. Han pleaded with Babba to let them go. Jabba grined and ordered Han killed. Then Jabba turned to the beautiful young princess and commanded, "Bring her to me." He laughed his lustful laugh as Leia is brought before him. Leia tried to talk to him about the future consequences of what he is doing: "We have powerful friends. You're gonna regret this." But Jabba would not listen. He was only concerned about the moment—about what felt good then and there.

It was a sad mistake. Her powerful friend Luke returned. Leia was freed. Jabba's and his barge disappeared in a giant explosion. There was nothing left of him to bury or remember. The Tempter enticed Jabba to think about the instant gratification of sex, power, and wealth. He forgot about tomorrow.

The English poet, John Dryden, urged his readers to think ahead and to think of what the consequences of their acts will be, "Better shun the bate than struggle in the snare."

Another poet put it this way:

> You only thought
> you got away.
> But in the night
> you'll pay and pay.

The Christian Apostle James, like Luke Skywalker, was focused on a long range goal. He wrote: "Blessed is the man that endures temptation: for when he is tried, he shall receive the crown of life, which the Lord has promised to them that love him" (James 1:12). James would not sacrifice his future for a moments pleasure the Tempter might give him.

Run with the
right crowd

Luke Skywalker picked the wisest and the best for his companions. He lived on a farm with his Aunt Beru and his Uncle Owen, who were fine, hard working people. Only after they were dead did he leave. Then, his close friend was Ben, the most powerful member of the good Force. Later he went to spend his time with the great teacher of the good Force, Yoda. Even his two robot friends Threepio and Artoo were good astrorobots.

John Casper Lavater, a Swiss scholar, said, "You may depend on it that he is a good man whose intimate friends are all good, and whose enemies are decidedly bad." These two things could well be said of Luke Skywalker.

The Tempter first tries to put a person into a crowd of friends like he wants them to become. This is why the Bible warns: "My son, if sinners entice you, consent you not. If they say, Come with us...Cast in your lot among us...My son, walk not you in the way with them; refrain your foot from their path: For their feet run to evil" (Proverbs 1:10,11, 14-16).

Study hard

Luke studies the forces of good and bad under Yoda, the instructor who had trained Ben. Here is an example of Yoda's instruction to Luke:

> **YODA:** Run! Yes. A Jedi's strength flows from the Force. But beware of the dark side. Anger . . .

fear ... aggression. The dark side of the Force are they. Easily they flow, quick to join you in a fight. If once you start down the dark path, forever will it dominate your destiny, consume you it will, as it did Obi-Wan's apprentice.

LUKE: Vader. Is the dark side stronger?

YODA: No... no... no. Quicker, easier, more seductive.

LUKE: But how am I to know the good side from the bad?

BEN: Luke, don't give in to hate—that leads to the dark side.

YODA: Strong is Vader. Mind what you have learned. Save you it can.

Luke learned well. Later an enemy would say, "Obi-Wan has taught you well. You have controlled your fear."

Luke studied the spiritual Force. Likewise, the Bible tells us to, "Study to show thyself approved" (II Timothy 2:15). And the book for winners is the Bible. The Psalmist said, "Your word have I hid in my heart, that I might not sin against you" (Psalms 119:11). This is the way to keep the Tempter from defeating you. Study the Bible. Memorize the Bible. It is a manual on victory.

Stand on your own two feet

Luke learned that to defeat the Tempter he had to stand alone and take full responsibility. *Star Wars* producer George Lucas said: *"As* you're building to the climax of an endeavor such as this, you want the situation to get more and more desperate and you want the hero to lose whatever crutches he or she has helping along the way. One of the challenges here is that Luke should be completely on his own. He has to face the Emperor one on one."[27]

The present world lesson here is, "take responsibility." Stop depending on other people to help you overcome the Tempter. Look at the defeated souls who blame everything on others. They say, "My parents didn't have time for me or I would not have strayed;" "I wouldn't have done those things if I had not fallen in with the wrong crowd;" "I was stressed out and didn't think about what I was doing."

Pontius Pilate, the judge who tried Jesus, "Took water, and washed his hands before the multitude, saying. I am innocent of the blood of this just person: see you to it" (Matthew 27:24). Pilate refused to take responsibility.

Trust in the good Force

Luke's instructor, Yoda, urged him to "Remember, a Jedi's strength flows from the Force." His lightsaber was taken away. His spacecraft broke down. His friend Ben died. But these were not his strength. "A Jedi's strength flows from the Force."

George Lucas and Leigh Brackett discussed the different levels of the Force. They rated Ben as a six, Vader a four, and Luke is now at level two.[28] That was during *The Empire Strikes Back*. But by the final film, *Return of the Jedi*, Luke has studied under Yoda and learned from many conflicts to put more faith in the unseen. His power became much stronger.

The ancient Psalmist sang of his dependence upon the power of God and the victory that resulted: "You art my King, O God...Through you will we push down our enemies: through your name will we tread them under that rise up against us. For I will not trust in my bow, neither shall my sword save me. But you have saved us from our enemies, and have put them to shame that hated us" (Psalms 44:4-7).

Jesus Christ offers this supernatural power to all who will invite Him into their hearts. He promised, "But as many as received him, to them gave he power to become the sons of God, even to them that believe on his name" (John 1:12). He can give the weakest person the power to overcome the Tempter: "My strength is made perfect in weakness" (II Corinthians 12:9).

Never underestimate the seducer

Yoda told Luke, "Do not . . . Do not underestimate the powers." The following Bible story is about a young man who underestimated the power of the Tempter:

> "I discerned among the youths, a young man void of understanding, Passing through the street near her corner; and he went the way to her house, In the twilight, in the evening, in the black and dark night: And, behold, there met him a woman with the attire of an harlot, and subtle of heart. (She is loud and stubborn; her feet abide not in her house: Now is she without, now in the streets, and lies in wait at every corner.) So she caught him, and kissed him, and with an impudent face said unto him, I have peace offerings with me; this day have I paid my vows. Therefore came I forth to meet you, diligently to seek your face, and I have found you. I have decked my bed with coverings of tapestry, with carved works, with fine linen of Egypt. I have perfumed my bed with myrrh, aloes, and cinnamon. Come, let us take our fill of love until the morning: let us solace ourselves with love. For the goodman is not at home, he is gone a long journey: He has taken a bag of money with him, and will come home at the

day appointed. With her much fair speech she caused him to yield, with the flattering of her lips she forced him. He goes after her straightway, as an ox goes to the slaughter, or as a fool to the correction of the stocks; Till a dart strike through his liver; as a bird hastens to the snare, and knows not that it is for his life. Hearken unto me now therefore, O you children, and attend to the words of my mouth. Let not your heart decline to her ways, go not astray in her paths. For she has cast down many wounded: yea, many strong men have been slain by her. Her house is the way to hell, going down to the chambers of death" (Proverbs 7:7-27).

Note the genius of the Tempter who directed the young man's fall. The woman was aggressive. She ran up to him in the street, caught him, and kissed him. He thought, "I am simply irresistible. She cannot restrain herself."

This woman was clothed in the righteous garments of religion: "I have peace offerings with me; this day have I paid my vows." She has just come from paying her vows at church. This means the simple young man should feel no guilt and fear no punishment from God.

Her lines flattered her prey: "Therefore came I forth to meet you, diligently to seek your face, and I have found you." He thought himself the only one who could possibly satisfy the longing of her heart. He is it!

The temptation was made to appear safe. She assured him her husband was away and would not arrive to surprise them: "For the goodman is not at home, he is gone a long journey."

The allurement is increased by the fact she is no cheap woman. Doesn't her husband have a large bag of money with him on his travels? "He has taken a bag of money with him, and will come home at the day appointed."

The Tempter scripted her lines well, for: "With her much fair speech she caused him to yield, with the flattering of her lips she forced him." He goes to her straightway, without hesitation. The poor deceived prey does not realize she has had many guest before him. They are in hell, as he soon shall be. The Tempter won.

When Luke, Han and Leia land, Lando betrays them.
He leads them right into a trap—the room where
Darth Vader awaits them. Lando turns to his
old friend Han and says, "I'm sorry."
—The Empire Strikes Back

Chapter 11
THE PHANTOM'S MIND GAME

The most subtle of all weapons is the mind game. In *Star Wars*, the weapons that got all the attention were the lightsabers, the blasters, and the deadly space ships. But there was another mysterious and deadly one. The dark Force uses psychological warfare to slay its enemies with guilt.

The evil dark Force is a master of accusation. The Bible calls him "The Accuser." He struts into heaven and accuses men to God: "The accuser of our brethren is cast down, which accused them before our God day and night" (Revelation 12:10). Get this name: the "Accuser" He invades the conscience telling men how inferior and no good they are. He told God Job wasn't sincere and then told Job he was a hypocrite" (Job 1:9-11, 20:5).

The Accuser has the ability to explode a person's conscience and leave it in searing flames. John Crowne, the English dramatist, said, "There is no hell like a bad conscience." Socrates described a man's conscience as the wife from whom there is no divorce. Isaiah portrayed the trouble of an accused soul like this: "But the wicked are like the troubled sea, when it cannot rest, whose waters cast up mire and dirt. There is no peace... to the wicked" (Isaiah 57:20-21).

A guilty conscience strips us of confidence, saying, "After what you have done, you do not deserve to be a success and you certainly don't deserve to be happy."

The Accuser overwhelms people with fear, declaring, "You did it and you're going to pay." Shakespeare said, "Thus conscience does make cowards of us all."[29] The Bible says, "The wicked flee, when no man pursues" (Proverbs 28:1).

Guilt can wreck your health with its accusations. A West Texas store manager told me he had an affair with his wife's best friend while they were in college. His wife did not know, but he did. Though it had been many years in the past, he said it had driven him to the point he could not sleep at night and for days he had not been able to keep food down. Psalms 38:3-4,10 says, " my iniquities are...an heavy burden they are too heavy for me...my strength fails me."

Guilt can drive us to the brink of insanity. Dr. O. Hobart Mowrer said, "Mental illness can stem from cheating on income tax or anything that one has done and is afraid of being found out." One psychiatrist said, "Ninety percent of all the people in America's mental institutes could go home well if they could only accept forgiveness."

The Accuser can use guilt to make us hate our life and even drive us to destroy our life, as Judas did.

Star Wars gives six gigantic lessons for dealing with

the Accuser and his weapon of guilt.

How to deal with guilt
after a lover's quarrel

Han feels guilty after a lover's quarrel with Leia. In *Return of the Jedi,* Leia is standing in the moonlight outside the Chief of the Ewoks' hut. She is very emotional because Luke has just told her they are brother and sister. Han comes out of the chief's hut and asks Leia, "Hey, what's goin' on?" She replies "Nothing—I just want to be alone for a little while." Han becomes angry and demands she tell him what the trouble is. Leia replies, "I...I can't tell you." Then Han looses his temper and lets his jealousy show, "Could you tell Luke?" Han starts to walk away from her. But then he feels guilty and apologizes. "I'm sorry," Han says, as he gathers her tightly in his embrace.

The final *Star Wars* movie ends with Han and Leia embracing. He has finally learned he doesn't have to be jealous of Luke because he is her brother. The audience assumes their relationship will go on. But, if Luke had not said, "I'm sorry" and she had not forgiven him, the relationship might have been forever lost. Then Luke would have had to listen to the Accuser condemning him for the rest of his life.

The lesson here is that humans are not perfect. To hold on to a relationship, people have to be willing to apologize, as Han did, and forgive as Leia did. This is the key to success: "And be you kind one to another, tenderhearted, forgiving one another, even as God for Christ's sake has forgiven you" (Ephesians 4:32).

Dealing with guilt regarding past failures

In *The Empire Strikes Back,* Ben has to deal with guilt. Years before he was training a young Jedi. But the trainee was overcome by the dark Force and became the evil Darth Vader! As Luke gets ready to fly off and fight Vader, Ben says, "Luke, I don't want to lose you to the Emperor the way I lost Vader." Ben takes responsibility for this loss: "When I first knew him, your father was already a great pilot. But I was amazed how strongly the Force was with him. I took it upon myself to train him as a Jedi. I thought that I could instruct him just as well as Yoda. I was wrong." The Accuser blames Ben for Vader's fall. Ben reveals his guilt when he said, "I was wrong." But he did not give up. Ben fought back.

The lesson is we have to deal with past failure if we are to win. The first thing to do is realize everyone fails. Ben has more of the good Force than anyone in *Star Wars*, yet he had failures. So must we all. And we deal with it by trusting Christ for forgiveness and cleansing, "Bless the LORD, O my soul, and forget not all his benefits: Who forgives all your iniquities" (Psalms 103: 2-3).

We must remember failure isn't final. Ben did not give up, he got up. And in the end he won.

How to handle the guilt that comes from criticism

Luke has to deal with some very unfriendly creatures that didn't like him. In *Star Wars: A New Hope*, Luke is told that a giant savage-looking Wookiee doesn't like him, after giving Luke a rough shove. Luke apologizes, saying, "I'm sorry." The human replies, "I don't like you either." Luke tries to leave, but a blow from the unpleasant human sends him sailing across the room and crashing into tables. Then the human draws a chrome-plated pistol and aims it at Luke's friend Ben. In a flash Ben fires a laser beam that cuts off the human's arm.

This is a good lesson on how to deal with thugs who are determined to start fights. Luke turns the other cheek and apologizes when a man says he doesn't like him. Even though the problem turns dark and a bully's arm is cut off, Luke's conscience is clean. He did all he could to avoid a fight.

In this present world we have to deal with bullies. The best way to do this is to refrain from getting mad and starting something. Had Luke done this it could have ended with several people dead. Then the great Accuser would have hammered him with guilt for causing the deaths. When Luke was shoved and told he wasn't liked, he merely said, "I'm sorry."

Jesus said, "But I say unto you, That you resist not evil: but whosoever shall smite you on your right cheek, turn to him the other also" (Matthew 5:39). This way we don't have to suffer from guilt.

What to do when feeling guilty
over not graduating

Luke decided to leave school. At the command of Ben he had gone to study under Yoda. He was being trained in how to use the power of the good Force. This prepared him for a successful career as a Jedi warrior. It would help him fight the evil Empire. But Luke learns new facts about Darth Vader and is compelled to rush to battle. Yoda, his teacher, says, "Unfortunate that you rushed to face him...that incomplete was your training." Luke replies, "I'm sorry" and leaves for the battle front. But he continues his education by listening to the instructions of Ben.

Here are good lessons in how to deal with failure to graduate. First, Luke is not antagonistic with his teacher. He apologizes, saying, "I'm sorry." Second, he doesn't give up and say, "I can't ever do big things because I didn't finish my education." Third, he continues his on-the-job training. And in the end, Luke emerges as a well-learned *Star Wars* winner.

How to handle guilt
over betraying a friend

Lando had to deal with his awful betrayal of a friend. The evil Darth Vader knew Luke and Han were going to see Lando at Cloud City on the planet of Bespin. Vader flies there immediately and makes Lando lead Luke into a snare. When Luke, Han and Leia land, Lando betrays them. He leads them right into a trap. Lando turns to his old friend Han and says, "I'm sorry." But the damage is done. It appears Vader will kill them. Fortunately, they got away. But, the Accuser can jump on Lando for the rest of his life, telling him what a no good traitor he is.

However, Lando apologized and worked hard at being Han's very best friend to the end. The lesson is when we have betrayed a friend we must face them and say, "I'm sorry." Then we must not give in to guilt and quit.

What to do when inadequacy
makes us feel guilty

Lando is working hard to make up for his betrayal of his friend Han. He is going behind Darth Vader's back to try and help Han and his friends escape from the Empire. There isn't much he can do at this point but warn them of Vader's plans. Han says, "You fixed us all real good, didn't you? Then he hits Lando. "Stop!" says Lando. "I've done all I can. I'm sorry I couldn't do better, but I got my own problems." At this point Lando had to face his inadequacy. There is so little he can do. But he apologized again and stayed with it. In the end he is able to free Leia, Chewie, and Threepio. And finally, Lando rescues Han after he had been frozen and flown away by Boba Fett, the bounty hunter.

We learn here how to deal with the Devil's accusation that we are inadequate. We will always face situations in which we will feel we are not good enough. We aren't as athletic as some. Others may be better looking. Our grades may be inferior. We don't live in as big a house or drive as big a car as others. We may have fewer friends than some. Perhaps we do not make as much money as our peers. We may face family problems we don't seem able to solve. These are situations where the dark Accuser will try to drown us in guilt. His voice will echo in our mind, "You are inferior." Shakespeare's King Richard cried, "My conscience has a thousand several tongues, and every tongue brings in a several tale; And every tale condemns me for a villain."

We must face the dark Accuser with boldness just as Lando did and with the confidence of the Christian Apostle Paul who said, "I can do all things through Christ which strengthens me" (Phillipians 4:13). Everyone had to face the Accuser and his laser charged bolts of guilt. The key to winning is to learn how to say I'm sorry, get up, and move on.

The three steps to winning over the Accuser

We can win over the Accuser in all situations by following three simple steps.

First, make a complete confession of your faults. I John 1:8-9 tells us, "If we say that we have no sin, we deceive ourselves, and the truth is not in us. If we confess our sins, he is faithful and just to forgive us our sins, and to cleanse us from all unrighteousness."

Second, get honest and repent. Stop deceiving yourself by saying, "If my parents were not unreasonable, I would not have to lie to them. I have no sin. If my boss paid me what

I am worth, I wouldn't loaf on the job and steal from the cash register. If they had not mistreated me, I wouldn't hate them. If my mate gave me the affection I deserve, I wouldn't have to cheat." Get honest. Take full responsibility. Confess "I have sinned. It was totally my fault." Now, I am going to change.

Third, trust Christ's cleansing power. Just claim this promise: "If we walk in the light, as he is in the light...the blood of Jesus Christ his Son cleanses us from all sin" (1 John 1:7). There is one place your past can be changed; there is one place history can be rewritten—at the Cross of Calvary. It is good to be forgiven. It is better to be cleansed. The glory of the Cross is it takes away our past and gives us a real future. We must face life boldly, declaring we are clean. Because God says "the blood of Jesus Christ his Son cleanses us from all sin, we can boldly say, "I am clean from all sin."

Don't you love to get a past due notice when you have paid the bill? You don't do this by phone. You go down to the business, get the manager, stick your receipt in his face, and say, "Read this. It says "paid." I don't want one more phone call or letter. Do you understand? It has been paid." This is the way to deal with guilt. We must stick the receipt of Calvary in Satan's face and boldly declare, "I don't want to hear about this any more. The debt for my sins has been paid!"

The Accuser wins one

The *Associated Press* reported that skydiver John Wasik stepped from an airplane on a Sunday afternoon at 3,200 feet above Rockledge, Florida. Instead of gripping the ripcord he merely folded his hands in prayer. Terry Alford, the jump master for the local club, screamed at him to pull the chute. But his hands stayed folded in prayer. On the ground, Lyle Goodin, safety officer for the Falling Stars Jump Club, watched through binoculars. He followed him all the way down to the ground. Wasik never pulled the cord on either of his two chutes. They found a signed contract for his own funeral on John's body. He meant to die.

Why? Why didn't he pull the cord? Five weeks earlier, almost to the hour, Wasik stood in Green Air Park and watched his beautiful 22-year-old wife, Rickie, bail out of the same plane on her second jump. Her chute got tangled. Rickie died at her husband's feet.

For the next five weeks John had been tortured by the Accuser. He had been told over and over that it was his fault. He had killed his wife. John Wasik couldn't stand the guilt any longer. He tried himself, sentenced himself, and executed himself.

The Accuser loses one

For 20 years she had suffered at the hands of the fallen Phantom's ceaseless accusations. Guilt had wrecked her life—finally it threatened to end it. I first met her in Fort Walton Beach, Florida. She told of being forced to live with a sick aunt after her parents died. As a young teen-ager her new home was furnished with misery. She had to do all the housework, cook, care for the bed-ridden old lady and endure her ceaseless complaints and ruthless criticism. One day as she was helping her aunt up so she could change the sheets on her bed, the taunts became unbearable. She stepped back and let her aunt fall. The old lady's hip broke. Shortly after she died. The guilt ridden teenager cried, "I killed her. It was my fault." No body listened. They said, "Don't blame yourself. You were wonderful to her."

The pain of conscience became worse than the aunt's demands. She went wild, trying to drink and party her guilt away. It didn't work. Then she went off to college, disciplined herself to study, and made straight "A's." But her conscience still gave her an "F." Marriage, children, and a fine home could not relieve her misery. As her guilt began to threaten her sanity, she went to a psychiatrist who told her she had a guilt complex and had to quit blaming herself. She couldn't.

Finally, she discovered a way out. The Bible promised forgiveness and cleansing for guilty sinners. She asked Christ to do this for her. He did. The first stop she made afterwards was at the psychiatrist's office. She gleefully exclaimed, "You showed me the problem. Christ has shown me the solution." From that moment every day has been Christmas.

"Guilt upon the conscience, like rust upon iron, both defiles and consumes it," declared Englishman Robert South. But in contrast, a cleansed conscience can bring us a wonderful aid to a winning life.

God pleads with us to wake up to how Satan is wrecking our lives with his accusations and accept His cleaning: "Come now, and let us reason together, says the LORD: though your sins be as scarlet, they shall be as white as snow; though they be red like crimson, they shall be as wool" (Isaiah 1:18).

The winners in *Star Wars* were not perfect people. But they were able to go on in spite of their failures and inadequacies.

Commander: Holding her is dangerous...
She'll die before she'll tell you anything.
Vader: Leave that to me.
—Star Wars: A New Hope

Chapter 12

SLAVES OF THE DARK KINGDOM

The dark Force is not satisfied with our service—it wants slaves. *In Episode I, The Phantom Menace,* Darth Maul was set upon controlling. In *Star Wars: A New Hope.* Princess Leia was captured and held by Darth Vader aboard the giant Imperial starship. The beautiful young 16-year-old Princess was led down a low-ceiling hallway by a squad of armored stormtroopers. They bound her hands. Then she met the fearsome giant Darth Vader. Vader wanted to gain absolute control over her. He was determined to make her tell where the Rebel base was and where the plans were which showed how his ship could be destroyed. Vader said, "You are a part of the Rebel Alliance...and a traitor. Take her away! The Imperial soldiers began a brainwashing designed to give

Vader possession of her mind and soul.

The brainwashing strategy Vader put into action is the same one the dark Force is using in our world today. It enables the Force to completely possess humans. People have chosen a strange, but accurate, name for these slaves of the dark Kingdom. They call them "demon possessed."

In 28 A.D. a demon-possessed man was living in a cemetery and neighboring mountains in Gadara. This slave of Satan was in extremely bad condition after a long period of possession. It was evident that he was entering the final stage before termination. The Slave Reports gave these details.

Slave Report 1: Extreme misery

The slaves record showed he had grown extremely miserable in his confinement: "And always, night and day, he was in the mountains, and in the tombs, crying" (Mark 5:5).

His case was much like that of a California beach boy I once talked with. He had become a slave after wandering into Devil worship. It appeared he was not handling his bondage well. The handsome young man said he was so miserable that he didn't want to go on living.

The people that talked with him were puzzled by the young man's misery. They did not know what control the dark Force had over him. So they wondered why a handsome, personable, young man was so miserable. Of course, the Kingdom of the dark Force does not tolerate happiness among its slaves. It wants to see them suffer.

Slave Report 2: Sanity failing

The Gadara slave was lapsing into a severe state of insanity. Humans had concluded he was stark, raving mad. This is common.

Jack Roper of Milwaukee, Minnesota, did a study on

people involved with the dark Force. He noticed this: "When I am asked to meet with people who have been in Satanism, the places I meet them at are mental institutions." Many others in the mental institution are also slaves who had been taken over by drugs, sex, guilt, etc.

Slave Report 3: The slave was destitute, he had nothing

Lucifer stripped the Gadara prisoner of everything, even his clothes. The report shows this slave was completely destitute. Some people are surprised when they see people lose everything because they do not understand Satan's strategy. As often as it happens they fail to get the message.

The Soviet Union is a good example of what the Devil can do to wreck people financially. He used a slave named Karl Marx to strip a nation and leave its people destitute. Marx actually looked into becoming a Christian before joining the dark Force. But, shortly after finishing high school he wrote in a poem, "I wish to avenge myself against the One who rules above."[30] Later he took another step down the dark road and became a Satan worshipper. Marx went on to help lead the Soviet Union to renounce God and become an official atheist state. This resulted in the nation going broke and the people living in poverty.

In 1998, during the richest time in the history of the richest nation, the United States, 1.8 million went bankrupt. The Dark Kingdom controls its slaves and can take away their possessions at will, even in wealthy times.

Slave report 4: Prisoner becoming extremely violent

The prisoner in Gadara grew increasingly violent. The

slave report showed: "no man could bind him, no, not with chains: Because that he had been often bound with fetters and chains, and the chains had been plucked asunder by him, and the fetters broken in pieces: neither could any man tame him" (Mark 5:3-4). When other humans tried to restrain him, they failed. They put chains on him and he broke them. He was violent—completely out of control.

People are appalled at the violence of those possessed by the dark Force. When Satan yanks their restraints and shocks their brains they go wild. They join violent gangs. Their passions rage out of control. They rob, plunder, destroy, and kill strangers without reason. Their violence terrifies earthlings. The prisoner in Gadara was just one of millions, ready to explode when the dark Force commanded.

On April 20, 1999, two young men stormed into Columbine high school in Littleton, Colorado with guns and explosives, killing 15 people. Survivors said the pair, dressed in black trench coats, laughed and hooted as they opened fire on their classmates. Crystal Woodman, a junior, said, "They were just, like they thought it was funny. They were just, like 'Who's next? Who's ready to die?' They were just, like, 'We've waited to do this our whole lives.' And every time they'd shoot someone, they'd holler, like it was, like, exciting."[31] Students said the boys, part of a group called the "Trenchcoat Mafia," were fascinated with the Nazis and noted that the killings were carried out on Hitler's birthday.

Authorities were seeking an explanation for the two killers who committed suicide following their rampage. Governor Bill Owens said, "This is a cultural virus...We have to ask ourselves what kind of children we are raising," blaming society and parents. President Clinton rushed a note of sympathy to the community and victims in which he said, "We do know that we must do more to reach out to our children and teach them to express their anger and to resolve their conflicts with words, not weapons," indicating the problem was a lack of teaching. Other experts find a lot of answers to the question of why the young men killed: lack of supervision, accessible guns, a culture filled with violence, permissive or absent parents, TV and movie violence, and school officials who fail to act on warning signs. But nobody mentioned Satan. Not even a whisper was heard about the possibility of a supernatural dark Force acting upon the killers. One of the students said, "We always lived in sort of a sheltered situation. But now we realize that the world has hatred and evil that we didn't understand before this." This massacre brought us face to face with evil—Satanic evil.

Richard Ramirez was a killer with definite Satanic involvement. California's Night Stalker was charged with 13 counts of murder and 30 other crimes including rape, assault, and robbery. One of his victim's eyes were gouged out. Another told how Ramirez raped her after killing her husband. He forced some of his victims to "swear to Satan." During his pretrial hearing Ramirez shouted "Hail Satan" in court and held up his hand to show a Satanic pentagram on his palm. Investigator Robert Simandl, of the Chicago Police Department said, Ramirez "tried to join a Satanic group. They wouldn't let him in because the Satanists thought he was too weird so he started his own group."[32]

Ramirez spray painted pentagrams on the walls of the homes he ransacked. The El Paso, Texas resident, would stalk his victims by day and ravage them by night. Usually he would creep into their houses between midnight and 6:00 A. M. to attack them.[33]

Friends of the killer said the music of the Australian rock group AC/DC fascinated him. His favorite tune, "Night Prowler," from the album *Highway to Hell* was an outline for

Ramirez's killings: "You won't feel the steel until it's hanging out your back. I am your night prowler, I sleep in the day. Suspended animation, as I slip into your room. There ain't nothing you can do." Ramirez left a baseball cap with the AC/DC logo in the California condominium where he killed Dayle Okazaki. [34]

Following his death sentence for murder, Ramirez said, "Big deal. Death comes with the territory. See you at Disneyland." [35] He was not only willing to kill for Satan, but had no remorse about doing it.

Slave report 5: Prisoner is suicidal

The man in Gadara's mountain cemetery became suicidal. His slave report showed, "Night and day, he was... cutting himself with stones" (Mark 5:5). It was obvious the prisoner was being moved into the suicide zone.

When Satan is through using a slave he often enjoys terminating them. *The Washington Post* said an American teenager commits suicide every 90 minutes. Many of these are as a direct result of Satan taking control of their lives.

The following words were written by a 14-year-old who committed suicide. He wrote them in a diary he called the "Book of Shadows:" "To the Greatest Demons of Hell, I Tommy Sullivan, would like to make solemn exchange with you. If you give me the most extreme of all magical powers. I will kill many Christian followers who are serious in their beliefs. Exactly 20 years from this day I promise to commit suicide. I will tempt all teenagers on earth to have sex, have incest, do drugs, and to worship you. I believe that evil will once again rise and conquer the love of God."[36]

On January 9, 1988, Tommy murdered his mother with his boy Scout knife, arranged several occultic books in a circle, set them on fire, and attempted to burn up his father and his brother. At 9:30 the next morning they found Tommy in a blood-soaked snow bank. His wrists and throat were slashed. Tommy Sullivan kept his vow.

The dark Force desires to control every person. Random obedience does not satisfy him. He wants total possession of body, soul, and mind. The Gadara case clearly shows the Devil's three stage strategy for taking over a man's life. It is the same strategy used by Darth Vader to try and possess Princess Leia.

Possession strategy 1: Isolation

The first stage in gaining complete possession is to get the subject alone—to isolate them. Vader put Princess Leia in solitary confinement behind an electronic cell door where the young Princess was completely isolated.

Likewise, the man of Gadara was in the loneliest place in all the land—a cemetery for the insane. The people of the region were afraid to go near the spot. They thought demon spirits were in the cemetery. When he went there he was sure there would be no people coming around. He was totally isolated.

Loneliness is dangerous. The first observation God ever made about man was: "It is not good that the man should be alone; I will make him an help meet for him" (Genesis 2:18). Eve was seduced by the Serpent when she was away from her husband, alone. Ecclesiastes 4:10 warns, "Woe to him that is alone when he falls; for he has not another to help him up." Jesus was alone in the wilderness when the Tempter came to him. Hebrews 10:25 warns us not to forsake the "assembling of ourselves together."

Despite all these warnings, people allow themselves to become isolated. The State of the Nation's Housing, Harvard University Joint Center for Housing Studies, gives this report on the soaring number of isolated Americans:

Year	Total Households*	Single House*	Percent
1970	63.4	10.9	17
1980	80.8	18.3	28
2000	105.5	31.1	30

(* in millions)

The Harvard University's Joint Center for Housing Studies report said there were 11 million Americans living alone in 1970. In twenty years the number had soared to 24 million isolated Americans!

Two-and-one-half million American youth are classified as "disconnected." They do not have strong family ties, group ties at school, or a job where they are associating with other people.

Richmond detective Snowden explains how Satanists broke a child's relation with its mother: "One (Satanic) ritual...involves putting the child in an open coffin, lowering the coffin into a grave and throwing earth or blood on to the child. When it screams for his mother, who is present, the head priest removes the child from the grave. In this way the child learns who will come to his rescue—not his natural mother but the priest." His relationship with his mother is broken and he is well on the road to being a victim of Satanic control.[37]

The dark Force's strategy is to break every relationship. Children are urged to seek cars as soon as possible to get away from their parents. They are enticed to move away from home to college, instead of enrolling in home-town schools. Some are convinced to run away from home. Friendships are broken by betrayal. Employees are told the boss is bad and enticed to leave the company. Courtships are broken up over slight disagreements. Divorce is a popular way of settling family disagreements. People are discouraged from going to the church where they develop relationships.

The Devil's goal is to break every connection with parents, friends, dates, employers, mates, and fellow church members. Often people do not realize what is going on. They do not understand that Lucifer is constantly working to isolate them.

Possession strategy two: Humiliation

Stormtroopers opened the door to Princess Leia's cell, allowing Vader to enter. He said, "Your Highness, we will discuss the location of your hidden Rebel base." A black torture robot entered Leia's cell. It's mechanical hand carried a long hypodermic needle. The door slid shut. The humiliating things young Leia suffered are left to the imagination.

The second strategy the Devil used to possess the man in Gadara was humiliation. Lucifer did this by getting him to run around in public with no clothes on: "He ware no clothes" (Luke 8:27). If a person takes off their clothes and runs around town naked, it is going to be very difficult for them to ever return to a normal life. They will feel ashamed. They will not want to look their friends in the face. They might even think about killing themselves.

In Haiti, where the Devil is worshipped by 90 percent of the population, it is easy to see how humiliation is used. Satan degrades the voodoo worshippers by leading them into acts such as kissing dirt, drinking blood, and taking off their clothes and assuming lewd positions beside public roads. In 1957, at Bay de Heine, Haiti, a voodoo worshipper despised himself so, he took a machete and cut his legs off. In the same village a man was taken to the local clinic after cutting his abdomen open in five places. Nearly all Haitian suicides are "voodoo related." These people feel so dirty, so no good, they want to punish themselves and even kill themselves.

Humiliation makes people hate themselves. It makes them despise the parents who brought them into this world. And humiliation makes people detest the God who created them. This is exactly what Satan wants.

Possession strategy three : Indoctrination

Finally, Vader started indoctrinating Princess Leia. They told her she was going to die and the Rebel cause was lost. Governor Tarkin says: "Princess Leia, before your execution I would like you to be my guest at a ceremony that will make this battle station operational. No star system will dare oppose the Emperor now." Leia replies, "The more you tighten your grip, Tarkin, the more star systems will slip through your fingers." Tarkin says: Not after we demonstrate the power of this station. In a way, you have determined the choice of the planet that'll be destroyed first. Since you are reluctant to provide us with the location of the Rebel base, I have chosen to test this station's destructive power...on your home planet of Alderaan. Leia cries, "No! Alderaan is peaceful. We have no weapons. You can't..." But he does.

Here is the clear message they were telling Leia, "Our battle station is operational. We can destroy any planet we wish. We hold the power of life and death over you and the universe. It is useless to resist. You are in a completely hopeless situation. Surrender to the dark Force." All this proved to be a lie, but it was what Vader wanted to cram in her mind.

Satan's third phase of possession strategy is to fill the mind with things that are not true —to indoctrinate them. When the Gadara prisoner encountered Jesus Christ, he cried out, "What have I to do with you, Jesus, you Son of God most high? I beseech you, torment me not" (Luke 8:28). The Devil had convinced the man that Jesus was out to torture him.

I thought about the way they had told this prisoner lies about Jesus when a police detective gave me a copy of a Bible seized in an investigation of a Colorado teenager. The mind of the young man who owned the Bible had been filled with the lies of the Dark Kingdom. He had drawn a pentagram, a symbol of Satan on the cover of God's Word. He changed the words "Holy Bible" to "Unholy Bible." Inside the book he penned the words:

> "In all that you say,
> and all that you do,
> May the forces of Hell
> Always live with you."

He had changed the "do nots" of the Ten Commandments to read "do." He even wrote in the Bible that he denied Jesus Christ, calling Him a loser and the son of a whore. This youth crossed out the Lord's prayer and rewrote it as:

> "Our father who dwells in hell,
> unholy be his name.
> Their Kingdom will not come.
> His will, will not be done.
> Satan's kingdom will come.
> Satan's will, will be done on earth as it is in Hell!
> Lead us into temptation and deliver evil unto us.
> For thine is the power and
> the glory forever and ever.
> Hail Satan!"

The Satanic organization "CASH" (Continental Association of Satan's Hope) says, "Do not be tricked or fooled by the church and its lies." The Montreal-based international organization declares, "The whole goal of the church is to tear you down and make you feel inferior."

Their literature contains lies about Jesus:

1. The cross represents a man whose idea of success is death.
2. Forgiveness is a "ridiculous gospel." "After all, why should you not hate your enemies—if you 'love' and 'forgive' them does that not place you at their mercy? After all, why should you not hate your enemies—if you 'love' and always 'forgive' them does that not place you at their mercy? Does this not strengthen their position of power and yours of weakness?"
3. Hell" is a lie concocted to scare Christians into giving their money. "Throughout the years there is no lie or threat as great as the one 'If you give in to the temptations of the Devil you will surely suffer eternal damnation.'

Communists borrowed this strategy

The Communists in Korea and Vietnam used the dark Force's brainwashing strategy to bring prisoners under complete control. They would isolate their prisoners in solitary confinement. Some spent as much as six years alone. They would humiliate the prisoners by forcing them to tell publicly the worst thing they had done to their mother and their most terrible acts. After this they would play recordings over and over to indoctrinated them in the Communist lies. This was so effective some of the prisoners would not accept freedom when it came. They were convinced the Communists were right. They were totally possessed.

The program worked for Jim Jones

These three weapons of the evil Emperor were used

by Jim Jones to lead 912 people to commit suicide at his command. *Time* magazine asserted, "The most haunting image of 1978 was one of absolute stillness: row upon row of men, women and children, more than 900 of them, lying face down where they had died, many after swallowing a purple fruit drink laced with cyanide and served up from a metal vat."

How did Jim Jones possess these humans so completely that they would destroy themselves? First, they were cut off from family and friends. Dr. J. Thomas Ungerleider of the UCLA Neurophyshiatyric Institute said, "This wouldn't have happened if they hadn't been so isolated, with no feedback from the outside world."

Jones humiliated his followers in the worst ways. For punishment he would lower his members into a pit of human sewage. He would force his followers to perform shameful sexual acts. The shame made it hard to ever go back to a normal life.

During the nights preceding the mass suicide, Jones played recordings of his teachings an average of six hours a day. This taught them that God could not be trusted, only Jones was to be believed. The cult leader said he found that after this "They were nothing more than barnyard animals in my hands." He had absolute control over them. Jones even ordered them to kill their babies and take their own lives and they did it without question..

The liberation

In the *Star Wars* story Luke Skywalker's father gave him a lightsaber. This was unlike any other weapon in the universe and a symbol of Luke's destiny. Luke and Ben were on a mission in *Star Wars: A New Hope*. It included setting Princess Leia free. And free her they did. This was due in part to Luke's lightsaber.

Likewise, Jesus Christ was given a weapon by His

Father—the power of the Holy Spirit. It was a weapon from another era—the Holy Spirit. It is unlike any other in the world and a symbol of Jesus' destiny. It was the "Sword of the Spirit" Jesus depended on to free the slave in Gadara: 'The Spirit of the Lord is upon me...to preach deliverance to the captives" (Luke 4:18). The Spirit gave Him his power "to proclaim liberty to the captives, and the opening of the prison to them that are bound" (Isaiah 61:1).

When Christ and his disciples arrived in Gadara, the demon possessed man came running down a mountain and fell at Jesus' feet screaming. Christ commanded the demons to leave him and the slave of Gadara was set free. Christ's Holy Spirit power sent the demons into a herd of swine. They ran over a cliff and killed themselves.

When the people who lived nearby came out to see the disturbance, they hardly recognized the former slave. He was calmly sitting down. He had regained his sanity. And he even had clothes on. The Bible records: "The people of Gadara found him that was possessed with the devil...sitting, and clothed, and in his right mind" (Mark 5:15).

The former prisoner was so happy to be free, he told Jesus he would follow him anywhere. Christ sent him on a mission back to his home. He instructed the former slave of Satan to tell his friends at home how he had escaped by the power of Jesus Christ—power that could set them free also!

Deliverance from the dark Force

Jesus, by the power of the Holy Spirit, continues to set Satan's slaves free. The story of Sean Sellers is an example. He is spending his final days penciling poems and reflections in a spiral notebook. He is handsome, young, blonde, articulate, and personable. His good looks hide a past filled with unimaginable horrors.

Sean is on death row because of a passionate love affair; a love affair with the Devil. It began one day in school when a classmate gave a report on witchcraft. Sean was intrigued. He talked with her after school and soon became deeply involved in the occult. Dungeons and Dragons, demonic music, and Satanic rituals became his favorite pastimes.

Sean hid his Satanism at home, but he flaunted it at school. One day, in biology class, he drank a vial of fresh blood and ate the legs off a live frog. The young zealot displayed his faith in the devil by wearing his left sleeve rolled half way up and painting his long, pinkie fingernail jet black. In February, 1985, Sean wrote in his own blood, "I renounce God, I renounce Christ, I will serve only Satan." To prove his devotion, Sean vowed he would break all ten of God's commandments.

On the night of September 8, 1985, he completed that vow by murdering Robert Bower, a store clerk. Following this, Sean turned in a paper in English class which said, "Satan made me a better person. I am free. I can kill without remorse." His teacher was so alarmed she phoned Sean's mother. Immediately, his mother wrote a six-page letter to her son. In it she said, "Sean...I'll always love you...I'll always be here when you need me...until the day I die." She never dreamed that the day she wrote this would be the day she died.

That afternoon Sean came in from his part-time job at a pizza parlor and began his nightly ritual. He put on his black underwear, prepared an altar, and began worshipping Satan. Late in the night Sean slipped out of his room, killed his stepfather, and shot his mother to death while she slept.

Following Sean's death sentence on three counts of murder, Christian young people wrote Sean about God's love for sinners, even murderers. In his Oklahoma jail cell those letters and the Bible brought Sean face to face with Jesus Christ. One morning about daybreak he had a personal experience with Jesus. His life did a complete turn around.

The largest audience that had ever watched a TV documentary saw Sean Sellers on a Geraldo Rivera Satanism special. Geraldo did a good job of keeping the program on his track. He discussed the gruesome aspects of the problem without giving any answers. Then Sean Sellers came on boldly declaring, "There is no way out of Satanism except through Jesus Christ." Geraldo immediately broke for commercials. Before the program was over, Sean Sellers, speaking live by satellite from Oklahoma's death row repeated, "There is no way out of Satanism except through Jesus Christ."

Vader said, "When I left you, I was but the learner;
now I am the master." Ben replied, "You can't win Darth.
If you strike me down, I shall become more powerful
than you can possible imagine."
—Star Wars: A New Hope

Chapter 13

THE DEATH THAT ROCKED THE GALAXY

It is the puzzling paradox, good must die or evil wins. Ben who is the most powerful representative of the good Force in *Star Wars: A New Hope*, had to die for the wicked Darth Vader's forces to be defeated. Their battle took place aboard the gigantic space ship Death Star. Everything good in the universe hinges on the outcome. Ben boldly walked right down the corridors of the ship where Vader and a hostile army awaited him. Ben and Vader engage in a fight to the death. As their lightsabers hit together, lightning flashes, the Dark Lord of the Sith suddenly sweeps his saber around and cuts Ben in half.

Before his death, Ben made a promise to Vader, "You can't win Darth. If you strike me down, I shall become more powerful than you can possible imagine." This proved true. Ben's spirit came back and led Luke and the Rebels to victory.

In another era, thousands of years ago, a conflict raged between Jesus Christ who represented everything righteous and the evil Satan. The battle climaxed in the city of Jerusalem. Everything good was at stake. Jesus walked boldly into a city waiting to kill Him. There Jesus and Satan engaged in a battle to the death. As the heavens turned dark and the earth trembled, Jesus was cruelly killed on a cross.

Before his death Jesus made a promise to Satan that he could not win, "Destroy this temple, and in three days I will raise it up...he spoke of the temple of his body" (John 2:19, 21).

A long, long time before, God promised Eve that her seed would bruise Satan's head. Thousands of years later Jesus was born without an earthly father, the seed of the woman. Thirty-three years later He went quietly into the city where his enemies waited to kill Him. There He was crucified.

It was a terrible scene. Nature revolted. The earth quaked. The rocks were ripped in two. The sky grew black at noonday. The enemy appeared to have won. But, in a strange way Christ would come back from the grave with far more power. His Spirit would lead His disciples to victory.

A death reversed
evil's greatest victory

Darth Vader had just won a great victory in the first *Star Wars* movie. His great space ship Death Star directed a huge laser blast toward the planet Alderaan. The green planet is instantly blown up and turned into space dust. Vader is confident he can now rule the universe. With a touch of a button he can destroy any planet he wishes. No one will be able to stand against his Death Star. There is only one hope of stopping Vader. There are detailed plans of the ship which can reveal a weakness in Death Star that could be exploited. But they must get those plans.

Ben invaded the ship searching for them. He lost his life in the effort, but Luke got away with the plans. They showed him where the ship's weakness was. Following those plans Luke later fired a torpedo through the exhaust port into Death Star's main reactor. Against a blanket of stars the deadly Death Star bursts into a spectacular supernova and sent Vader's ship spinning off into space. Vader's great victory was reversed.

In the real war, Satan won his greatest victory in Eden. He seduced earth's first couple, Adam and Eve, to rebel against God. It destroyed the couple's paradise. It drove them from God's Holy Presence. Their sin brought a death penalty to them and to all their descendants. Satan appeared to have won.

But at Calvary Jesus died to pay the death penalty for Adam and all his descendants. The penalty of sin is death, and Christ paid that price so that humans could be reunited with their God. Against a sky darkened at noonday, Jesus destroyed the power of sin "That he might reconcile both unto God in one body by the cross" (Ephesians 2:16).

Former enemies of God are forgiven and restored to the Father. The prodigal can run back into the father's arms. Sinful people can be cleansed and made fit for God's heaven. The long separation is over: "And, having made peace through the blood of his cross, by him to reconcile all things unto himself; by him, I say, whether they be things in earth, or things in heaven" (Colossians 1:20).

Now, every time the message of the Cross brings a

human back to God, the Devil remembers Calvary and weeps over it.

The death that deceived the great Deceiver

In *Star Wars*, Vader thought sure the death of Ben spelled victory. He cut him and his robe in half. But when the robe fell to the floor it was suddenly empty. Ben's body disappeared. Later he would reappear and his voice would direct Luke to victory against the dark Force of Darth Vader.

Likewise the Devil thought he had won when Jesus was crucified. He had no way of knowing that Jesus would survive death and defeat him. The grave clothes that wrapped his body were suddenly empty. Jesus' body disappeared. But later He arose and reappeared. Every since He has been directing His church to victory over the dark powers of the Devil.

Dr. F. J. Huegel said, "However much others might have been deceived as to the true source of so much hate and such relentless cruelty, Jesus was not. The Pharisees were but tools, Judas was a tool, the Jews who cried "'crucify, crucify,' were but tools. Satan was the hand controlling those tools. It was to face him in mortal conflict that Jesus had come. "For this purpose the Son of God was manifested, that he might destroy the works of the devil" (I John 3:8). If the "prince of this world," Lucifer, had only know what defeat the cross would bring him he would never have instigated the crucifixion. The great deceiver had been deceived: "None of the princes of this world knew: for had they known it, they would not have crucified the Lord of glory" (I Corinthians 2:8).

The death that turn men from the dark Force

Solo, Chewie, Luke, and Leia were tensely watching as Ben died, in *Star Wars: The Last Hope*. Aghast, Luke screams out, "No." Ben had given his life fighting to deliver them and the plans that would save the universe from the dark Force. This sacrifice would change Luke forever. Later, under the great pressure to surrender Luke stood true to Ben's cause.

The disciples of Jesus watched intently as Jesus died on Calvary. They knew He had chosen to die to save them from the dark Force of Satan. His sacrifice would change men forever. Later the disciples would stand true to the cause of Christ, even when they faced martyr's deaths. And through the centuries Christ's sacrifice would draw millions to love Him and follow Him. It happened as Jesus said it would: "And I, if I be lifted up from the earth, will draw all men unto me. "This he said, signifying what death he should die" (John 12:32-33).

At the cross Jesus wrote the greatest love letters ever written in His own blood. It says, "I love you. I love you just like you are, I love you in spite of what you've done. I love you enough to give my life for you!" Calvary's love is a great power drawing people away from Satan to Jesus Christ.

Jesus' disciple Paul was attacked by the Devil in an effort to turn him to the dark side. Paul suffered rejection, ridicule, hatred, stonings, and imprisonment. But all the power of hell could not turn him back to the dark side. Calvary's love was the force that set Paul's affections on Jesus: "The Son of God, who loved me, and gave himself for me" (Galatians 2:20).

The death that set the prisoners free

In *Star Wars: The Last Hope*, Ben's invasion of Death Star cost him his life, but it freed Princess Leia. She was being held prisoner by the brutal Darth Vader aboard the ship Death Star where she was terrified by his threats. But Ben and Luke went into the evil ship after her. Ben lost his life in the battle, but Leia was set free.

Jesus invasion of earth cost Him his life, but it set many people free. In the Garden of Eden man was kidnapped by the Devil. But at Calvary Jesus paid the ransom price to have them released, "The Son of man came...to give his life a ransom for many" (Matthew 20:28). At the cross, Jesus Christ paid the ransom, so we can go free. No longer do we have to labor as a slave of Satan. No longer must we be held prisoner by drink, drugs, gambling, sex, greed, anger, hatred, jealousy, or unforgiveness." The ransom has been paid. Man can be free at last.

Satan must watch many of his slaves slip free of his bondage. The Cross has broken his evil grip and liberated them. But, just as following the Civil War some slaves chose to remain in their master's service, some of the dark Force's slaves choose to stay in his service. But no man has to remain. Now, all who choose can go free.

The death that
stripped away the mask of evil

When Darth Vader killed Ben he exposed how wicked he was. Ben was a good person. He had done nothing worthy of being cut in half for. It was the evidence needed to convict Darth Vader of wickedness beyond any doubt.

Likewise, when Satan enticed Judas to deliver up Jesus to be killed, he revealed how wicked he was. From that day he has been judged an evil being. Jesus said when he died, "The prince of this world is judged" (John 16:11). The crowds saw Pontius Pilate trying Jesus Christ. They heard the verdict "Guilty" echo throughout Jerusalem. But the generations that followed would judge Satan and find him guilty.

The cross showed what a completely evil force he is. He tortured and killed the humble, sinless Savior who brought nothing but love into the world. He brutally butchered the Lord who fed the hungry, healed the sick and taught people to love each other. Satan killed someone who prayed for His killers and even made an excuse for them: "Then said Jesus, Father, forgive them; for they know not what they do" (Luke 23:34).

At the Cross, the full wickedness of the Fallen Prince is exposed. There is only one verdict for Satan—"guilty." To the Devil and his servants, the world must say: "Him...you have taken, and by wicked hands have crucified and slain" (Acts 2:23).

At the cross Satan was stripped of his disguises. His true character is seen. Calvary shows him for what he really is—a liar and a murderer.

The death that
killed the killer

Ben's mission ended in death but it would serve to destroy the lethal ship Death Star. It would not be seen for a while. But Ben's mission obtained the plans that revealed the ships weakness and would lead to its destruction. Later Vader and the evil Emperor would be defeated. Vader would continue his evil work for a brief while. But it is all over. Ben and the good Force had won. Vader and Death Star are finished.

As Jesus approached his painful death on the cross, He declared, "Now shall the prince of this world be cast out" (John 12:31). This is good news to the human race. The "Prince of this world"—Satan—is cast out. Note the tense: "now." Jesus died and rose from the dead, "And having spoiled principalities and powers, he made a show of them openly, triumphing over them in it" (Colossians 2:15). Jesus, in death, triumphed over Satan.

At Calvary the serpent's head was bruised by a fatal blow. This is what God had promised. As a dead snake goes on twisting and turning, Satan continues his evil work for a while, but he is finished. When Christ's life blood flowed to the ground and it seemed all was lost, the Lord proclaimed, "It is finished!" His mission was completed. The evil Prince that cursed man in Eden is defeated! The reign of Satan is over!

The death that destroyed death

The powerful ship, Death Star, gave Darth Vader and the Emperor power to destroy planets and all the people on them. No one could possibly survive a laser which could turn a planet into dust. A death sentence was hanging over the galaxy. Ben's fatal mission changed all that. Death Star weakness was uncovered. It was later destroyed. The universal threat of death was removed. Later, when Ben's voice was heard and his body reappeared his followers knew he had escaped death. And thousands were delivered from the threat of Death Star's fatal beams.

The power of death was granted Satan in his victory in Eden. That power was demonstrated when Adam and Eve and their descendants died. Since then, no person could possibly survive death because the wages of sin are death and all have sinned. A death sentence was hanging over all people. Then Jesus went to the cross. His mission cost Him his life. But it destroyed the death penalty hanging over all humans. If a judge says you have to pay a $125 fine for breaking a traffic law and someone pays your fine, you do not have to pay it. The fine for our sins is death, but Christ went to the cross and paid it for us. So, we can go free.

Later, when Christ's voice was heard and His body reappeared, his followers knew He had escaped death:

"Forasmuch then as the children are partakers of flesh and blood, he also himself likewise took part of the same; that through death he might destroy him that had the power of death, that is, the devil" (Hebrews 2:14).

Satan's servants had a stone put over the entrance to Christ's grave. It was sealed with a Roman seal. Guards were placed there to see that the grave was not opened. But it was all to no avail. The soldiers were cast aside, the seal of mighty Rome was broken, and the huge stone rolled away. All the powers of Caesar and Satan were shattered. The Son of God rose triumphant!

"But now is Christ risen from the dead, and become the first fruits of them that slept. For since by man came death, by man came also the resurrection of the dead" (I Corinthians 15:20-21).

A death that still sets people free

Two millenniums later, the Cross is still giving people victory over the dark Force. Holly, a seventeen-year-old girl in north Louisiana, is living proof that Jesus' victory works today. Holly had always been a good, religious girl with a fine relationship with her parents. Then she met a new boyfriend. She did not know he was a Devil worshipper.

The boyfriend slowly led Holly into the world of Satan. They started playing "Dungeons and Dragons." She liked this because she was smart enough to beat other players. This game opened her mind up to a new supernatural power. Next the boyfriend started giving her drugs.

One night when Holly was high on drugs he took her to a meeting of Satan worshippers out in the woods. This really impressed Holly because many important community leaders were there. The Chief of Police was the grand master. There were two preachers and many professional people in

the group of 75. She joined in chants with the group. She watched as they drove nails through live cat's front paws to nail them to a tree. Then they skinned them alive from the neck down. The blood was caught and drank by the group. Holly said she was heavily drugged and afraid to refuse their demands. Then she watched as they went through sexual rituals.

Holly said there were outbursts of praise for those who had accomplished something good for Satan. If a boy had won a friend to the Devil, they applauded him and allowed him to pick any girl he wanted as a reward. At the end of the meetings they made work assignments to each member of the group.

Holly was usually given the responsibility of getting the drugs for the next meeting. She would spot a classmate pushing drugs at school, call the police chief and have them bust him. The police would confiscate the drugs. Later they would turn up at the Satanist meetings. Investigations collaborated Holly's story. The drugs were missing from police headquarters.

When the group, which had grown to 150, started talking about a human sacrifice, Holly was afraid and wanted to quit. They told her she couldn't. Holly was terrified.

Through two years of meeting with the Satanist, her relations with her parents had gotten worse and worse. Finally, they put down their foot and told her she had to go off to a summer Christian camp. Holly was furious. At the camp God started working in her life. A girl friend told her how she had left Satanism to become a Christian. Then a young preacher preached a sermon on Satanism. Holly said it, "was the story of my life. Every thing he mentioned, I had done." The preacher told how Jesus had died to set her free. Holly knew she had been wrong and decided to turn to Jesus Christ.

Holly felt an overwhelming sense of forgiveness for all her sins. The power of God became real in her life. She boldly informed the Satanists she was quitting, no matter what they did.

A barrage of threats started coming. Men appeared in the field around their house late at night. Harassing phone calls terrorized the family. Her former boyfriend put a gun to Holly's 13-year-old sister's head and said, "See how easily we can get your family." One night Holly's mother was awakened by a man who told her, "We are going to give you a sign of what will happen if your daughter talks." The next morning there was a dead cat on her mother's car seat. It had been cut up in a Satanic ritual.

Jesus gave Holly the courage to endure these threats. Today, her relationship with her parents is mended. She has learned how evil Satan is and how powerful Jesus is. Through Jesus' death Holly has been set free!

Never!...I'll never turn to the dark side.
You've failed, Your Highness.
I am a Jedi, like my father before me.
—Luke Skywalker

Chapter 14
UNLOCKING THE POWER OF THE FORCE

In the *Star Wars* story Ion blasters, lightsabers, high-energy gas blasters, and vibro-active force pikes are the weapons most noticed. If these aren't enough in *Episode I—The Phantom Menace*, Darth Maul banishes a double-bladed light saber. But there was another far more powerful than these—the supernatural power of the good Force. Ben and Luke knew how to use this potent weapon. They practiced boldly declaring their faith in the Force. In the fantasy wars, it was their words of faith that made them winners.

As Ben taught Luke to use the good Force, Jesus taught his disciples they could use God's supernatural power by boldly declaring their faith: "For verily I say unto you, That whosoever shall say unto this mountain, Be you removed, and be you cast into the sea; and shall not doubt in his heart, but shall believe that those things which he says shall come to pass; he shall have whatsoever he says" (Mark 11:23). When Christians boldly say to their mountainous barriers, "Be removed," and don't doubt in their heart. God's power will take away that barrier.

The one weapon Christians absolutely must have in their arsenal is this "word of faith." It is the key to the power of the good Force. In the book of Revelation, God says: "And I heard a loud voice saying in heaven, Now is come salvation, and strength, and the kingdom of our God, and the power of his Christ: for the accuser of our brethren is cast down, which accused them before our God day and night. And they overcame him by the blood of the Lamb, and by the word of their testimony; and they loved not their lives unto the death" (Revelation 12:10-11).

To overcome the super powerful evil Prince, man must depend on the blood Christ shed at the crucifixion on Calvary: "And they overcame him by the blood of the Lamb, and by the word of their testimony." Doubters ask, "If Satan is already defeated, how can he go on wrecking marriages, enslaving men, spreading crime and instigating wars?" The answer is the Devil can't; not alone. He must have the cooperation of the frail frightened humans who do not believe in the victory of Calvary.

An animal lesson

In the futuristic world of *Star Wars*, animals like the snowlizards and the furry Ewoks played an important part. In our war against Satan, animals can give us important lessons. It doesn't usually happen this way, but I saw it once. A big dog was chasing a terrified little cat. Her hair stood up straight. Her eyes nearly bulged out of her head. She ran for all she was worth. Unfortunately she just wasn't fast enough. Just before the big dog closed in to catch her and kill her, she stopped. The cat wheeled around, drew back its paw and screamed right in the dog's face. Suddenly the big dog lost all of his courage. He turned around, humped his back, and took off running, yelping every time his paws hit the ground.

I looked back at the cat sitting there licking its paw and thought, "You silly cat. What were you doing running in the first place? You had the victory won all the time and didn't know it."

Now how did the cat so dramatically reverse things and put the dog to flight? She just opened her mouth and gave the dog a word of testimony. She said, "Big boy you may kill me, but before you do, I am getting ready to claw your eyes out of your head. The dog thought about it and decided he'd rather run than fight. Now there is a Bible verse for the cat story: "Resist the devil, and he will flee from you" (James 4:7). If we resist Satan with our words of faith, he will flee and we will win.

The Devil's temptations, accusations and worries can be frightening. They can scare people into running away from their jobs, their business, their marriage, their dreams and ambitions, as well as the will of God for their lives. But The Devil cannot defeat Christians. All he can do is frighten, intimidate and chase them. To lose, a Christian must run. To win they must stop running and boldly tell the Devil they are not afraid of him, that he is a defeated foe, and that Jesus overcame him at the Cross. Christians are not working to victory— they are working from victory. It is already won.

The way to free yourself from fear

To practice the word of faith means we must forget about protecting ourselves. The cat was able to stop running

and give the dog his testimony when she got her mind on winning the fight instead of losing her life. The Bible says those
overcoming the Devil by the word of their testimony, "loved
not their lives unto the death" A winning warrior must love
victory, instead of loving himself. If we love our life, Satan
can threaten us, tempt us, and frighten us. But if we give up
our love for our selves, even "unto death," we can stand in
faith, boldly, and unafraid.

Jesus is looking for people willing to give up their ob-
sessive love for themselves: "And he that takes not his cross,
and follows after me, is not worthy of me. He that finds his
life shall lose it: and he that loses his life for my sake shall find
it" (Matthew 10:38-39). The humans who try to hide from the
Devil—who run from him, will in the end lose their lives.
Ironically those who give up their lives for Christ are the ones
who will preserve their lives.

In World War II the Japanese suicide pilots went to
the palace and participated in their funeral before beginning
their one-way bombing mission. This is what Christian baptism is, a funeral for a person who has given up their life to go
into battle against evil: "Know you not, that so many of us as
were baptized into Jesus Christ were baptized into his death?
Therefore we are buried with him by baptism into death: that
like as Christ was raised up from the dead by the glory of the
Father, even so we also should walk in newness of
life" (Romans 6:3-4).

George Mueller, a great warrior for Christ, ran a
home for orphaned children by "the word of faith." He never
told anyone of his financial needs. When he was asked the secret of his triumphant life, Mueller replied: "There was a day
when I died." He bent lower as he spoke, almost to the floor.
Then he explained, "Died to George Mueller, his opinions,
preferences, tastes, and will; died to the world, its approval or

censure; died to the approval or blame even of my brethren or friends; and since then I have studied only to show myself approved unto God."[38]

Star Wars author, George Lucas, said, "Heroes come in all sizes, and you don't have to be a giant hero. You can be a very small hero. Its just as important to understand that accepting self-responsibility for the things you do, having good manners, caring about other people—these are heroic acts. Everybody has the choice of being a hero or not being a hero every day of their lives. You don't have to get into a giant laser-sword fight and blow up three spaceships to become a hero." By declaring your faith, you can be a real world hero.

When facing the enemy, declare the victory!

In *Return of the Jedi*, when the Evil Emperor demands that Luke Skywalker yield to the dark side, Luke declared, "Never!...I'll never turn to the dark side. You've failed, Your Highness. I am a Jedi, like my father before me." Luke declared the victory and then he saw the victory.

When a little lad named David faced the nine foot giant Goliath in the war between Israel and the Philistines, he boldly declared, "You come to me with a sword, and with a spear, and with a shield: but I come to you in the name of the LORD of hosts, the God of the armies of Israel, who you have defied. This day will the LORD deliver you into my hand; and I will smite you, and take your head from you; and I will give the carcases of the host of the Philistines this day unto the fowls of the air, and to the wild beasts of the earth; that all the earth may know that there is a God in Israel" (I Samuel 17:45-46). David's faith enabled him to whip the giant and deliver his nation.

When your body fails, declare the victory!

In *A New Hope*, Threepio is hit by a large burst from Vader's laser fire. The droid's arms went limp. A high pitch noise comes from him and then dies out. Later, when they lifted his still form out of the space ship, it appears the little droid was finished. But Luke, in faith, announced, "He'll be all right." And he was restored to life!

The woman had an issue of blood that had taken away her strength, her youth, her health and now, her life. No doctor could help her. But one day she met Jesus and everything changed. "And a certain woman, which had an issue of blood twelve years, And had suffered many things of many physicians, and had spent all that she had, and was nothing bettered, but rather grew worse, When she had heard of Jesus, came in the press behind, and touched his garment. For she said, If I may touch but his clothes, I shall be whole. And straightway the fountain of her blood was dried up; and she felt in her body that she was healed of that plague....And he said unto her, Daughter, your faith has made you whole" (Mark 5:29-34).

Gypsie Smith, the Methodist evangelist, said, "There were many people that touched Jesus that day and nothing happened. But, this woman said, 'I'm going to touch Him and I shall be made whole.' And she was."

When facing temptations, declare the victory!

In *Return of the Jedi*, when the Evil Emperor demanded that Luke Skywalker yield to the dark side, Luke declared, "Never!...I'll never turn to the dark side. You've failed, Your Highness. I am a Jedi, like my father before me."

When Vader puts ever pressure on Luke to give in to the power of the dark side, Luke declares, "I will not turn."

When Satan tempted Jesus Christ to bow to him, Jesus boldly ordered, "Get you hence, Satan: for it is written, You shall worship the Lord your God, and him only shall you serve. Then the devil left him" (Matthew 4:10-11).

When face to face with impossible difficulties, declare the victory!

In *Star Wars: A New Hope,* the Rebels attacked the overpowering ship Death Star. All is grim. The Red Leader has been killed. There seemed to be no hope of victory. Everyone is ready to abandon the plan to go right into the ship and fire their torpedoes. Then Luke declares, "We're going in. We're going in full throttle." And he did, against impossible odds and won!

In *The Empire Strikes Back,* Luke leaves on a mission to save Han and Leia from death. His training is not complete. There seems little chance of Luke surviving, much less bringing his friends back. Yoda reminds him of how strong Vader, his enemy, is. Luke shows he has no doubt of victory. He declares, "I will. And I'll return. I promise."

Joshua stood before the impenetrable city walls of Jericho and declared his faith, "Shout; for the LORD has given you the city" (Joshua 6:16). The walls came crashing down and the Israelites rushed in to victory.

When the Apostle Paul faced impossible circumstances, he declared the victory, "In all these things we are more than conquerors through him that loved us" (Romans 8:37). Put a conqueror in jail and he will pick the lock, steal the key, dynamite the wall, and get out. Put Paul in jail, as they did in Phillipi, and he will not only get out, he will convert the jailer and send him out to preach the Gospel. Paul's faith made him more than a conqueror!

When your future hangs in the balance declare the victory!

In *Return of the Jedi*, the Emperor tells Luke, "In time you will call me master." Luke talked back to his powerful, evil enemy, "You're gravely mistaken. You won't convert me."

Likewise, when Lucifer is telling us in time he will be our master, that we cannot resist his temptations and cannot get to Heaven, we must tell him, "You're gravely mistaken." The Bible promises, "If you shall confess with your mouth the Lord Jesus, and shall believe in your heart that God has raised him from the dead, you shall be saved" (Romans 10:9). We can boldly tell Lucifer that we believe in Christ, we're confessing Him with our mouth and we shall be saved.

A little boy, seeking to win over evil, put his faith in Jesus Christ. He told his pastor, "The Devil keeps telling me I am not saved." The minister replied, "Every time these doubts come read I John 5:13, "These things have I written unto you that believe on the name of the Son of God; that you may know that you have eternal life." One night the lad was sitting in a chair reading this verse and he said, "The Devil kept sticking his head out from under his chair and saying, 'you're not saved'." The little boy said, "I finally got tired of it. I showed him the Bible and said, There it is Devil. Read it for yourself."

When facing death declare the victory

Old Ben, who taught Luke to rely on the good Force,

was locked in a death struggle with Darth Vader. As their laser swords cross in midair creating a low buzzing noise, Vader told Ben, "If you strike me down, I shall become more powerful than you can possibly imagine." Ben came back after death and lived on.

Jesus Christ promised His followers they would never die, "He that hears my word, and believes on him that sent me, has everlasting life, and shall not come into condemnation; but is passed from death to life" (John 5:24).

When Paul was facing death, he declared the victory, "We are confident, I say, and willing rather to be absent from the body, and to be present with the Lord" (II Corinthians 5:8). Paul declared he would live beyond the grave.

Get bold with the enemy and declare the victory

Jesus said it long ago: "Out of the abundance of the heart, the mouth speaks" (Matthew 12:34). When people talk to each other on the phone they can tell if the other party is excited, tired, happy, or worried. It is in their voice. Likewise, the Devil can detect fear or confidence by the way people speak. Winners practice boldly declaring the victory and Satan flees from them.

We have the right to boldly say to the Devil anything that God says: "For he hath said, I will never leave you nor forsake you. So that we may boldly say, The Lord is my helper, and I will not fear what man shall do unto me" (Hebrews 13:5-6).

Because God says, "My grace is sufficient for you: for my strength is made perfect in weakness" (II Corinthians 12:9), we can boldly say, "God's strength is being made perfect in my weakness." This is why the Bible commands: "Let the weak say, I am strong" (Joel 3:10).

Because God says, "In all these things we are more than conquerors through him that loved us," (Romans 8:37) we can boldly say to the Devil, "I am more than a conqueror though Jesus over all my fears, temptations, and trials."

A General's "word of faith" brings victory

Every man has a breaking point and during World War II General Wainwright finally reached his. On March 11, 1942, when General Douglas MacArthur departed for Australia, Wainwright took over command of all U. S. forces in the Philippines. The situation was already hopeless. On May 6, 1942, he was forced to surrender to the Japanese on Corregidor.

For the next three years he was a prisoner of war in Formosa and Manchuria. He was starved until he weighed less than 100 pounds. Finally, he had to face the fact that he was not going to make it. He was going to die in that prison— die without his family ever knowing what had happened to him. Then the tides of war changed and the Japanese surrendered. But no one had told the General. They went right on starving and abusing him.

Then, one day an American plane landed and a U. S. officer rushed into the concentration camp and cried, "General we've won. I am going on but they wanted me to tell you a plane is coming to pick you up. It's all over. We've won. The American officer flew away.

Later some Japanese officers return to the concentration camp that were not aware that General Wainwright had heard the news that he had won. When they started to abuse him, Wainwright ignored his frail body, threw his chest out and said, "I'm in charge. I'm taking command here." They wilted before him knowing he had heard about the victory.

Another plane carried the General to the U. S. Battleship Missouri in time to participate in the surrender ceremony. From there he returned to a hero's welcome and the home he had thought he would never see again.

Stand up to the dark Force and boldly say, "I am in charge. I'm taking command here now." Confront the dark Force with your testimony of faith and the good Force will work through you and give the victory.

*In a world where blaster bolts smell of ozone,
the darkness of the night is broken by the beams
of lightsabers and Tatoonine's canyons
hides mysterious eyes, special armor is essential.*

Chapter 15

SURVIVING LIGHTSABERS AND BLASTER BOLTS

In times of war, armor can make the difference between living and dying. The *Star Wars* soldiers wore high-tech armor for protection against the powerful weapons they faced: N-1 Naboo starfighters in *Episode I*, lightsabers, armored tanks (AATs) with noses strong enough to smash through walls.

In the many episodes of this future fantasy, wars are a constant part of life. In *Episode I* a battle rages between the Imperial troops and the Rebel forces. In the final episode a war erupts between Darth Vader and Luke Skywalker. It is a classic struggle caused by the unseen Force of good and the Force of evil.

One reason the *Star Wars* movies have captured a massive world-wide following is their focus on war. People are very conscious that life is a constant conflict in their personal, family, and business lives. They worry about winning.

Life is a war

The dark Force is out to devastate families, enslave their children, ruin their business, steal the affections of their mate, wreck their sanity, enslave them with bad habits, destroy their lives and damn their eternal souls. People can ignore the fight if they wish, but one day it will destroy them.

Life is a war. And, as William Tecumseh Sherman put it, "War is hell." And this is what life is—a fierce, hellish war.

The *Star Wars* struggle is really between two unseen forces—the evil dark Force and the good Force. A. T. Pierson, a Christian teacher, said, "There are two opposing hierarchies, eternally at war. Good angels in alliance with God, and all saints, to promote all that is good; evil demons confederate with each other and all evil men, to work disaster and ruin, and if it were possible, supplant even the Almighty."

Many Christians have forgotten that Jesus called on them to be soldiers. They focus on worship rather than warfare. They become entangled with the concerns of this life and forget about the battle with Satan. The Bible instructs us to: "Endure hardness, as a good soldier of Jesus Christ. No man that warreth entangles himself with the affairs of this life; that he may please him who has chosen him to be a soldier" (II Timothy 2:3-4). Every day must be an aggressive, relentless fight against evil.

The enemy is supernatural

Star Wars is a battle with the supernatural—with the

dark Force. Likewise, man faces Lucifer and his army of demons. We are locked in a life and death struggle with the dark force: "For we wrestle not against flesh and blood, but against principalities, against powers, against the rulers of the darkness of this world, against spiritual wickedness in high places" (Ephesians 6:12).

People are aware that life is a struggle, but seldom realize who he is struggling with. They like to think they are up against other humans—against "flesh and blood." For if they are only up against other people they feel confident and self-sufficient. If it is a human struggle they feels sure they "can handle it." So they blindly blame "flesh and blood" for all their problems.

- Their school teacher is hopeless. She doesn't have enough sense to get in out of the rain and here she is trying to teach them.
- Their trouble is with their mother-in-law. She just will not keep her nose out of their business.
- Their bad kids are just driving them crazy. Who would have ever thought those sweet little angels would turn out to be devils?
- The agents at the IRS are out to get them. If they don't put them in prison, they will surely put them in the poor house.
- The ruthless boss has no concern for them and no sense about how to run the job. He is driving them nuts.
- No-good politicians are ripping off their tax money and just using it to buy more votes. They are wrecking the country.
- Their wife is a mess. All she wants to do is

shop and nag. She is making life unbearable.

- Government officials are the problem. They keep imposing more and more restrictions on business. It is impossible.
- The Japanese are buying up their country, the Mexicans are taking their jobs and the Russians are ripping them off, and who is doing anything about it?
- Their mothers and dads are impossible parents. They do nothing but give orders, impose restrictions and then criticize them for being miserable failures.
- Loud-mouth neighbors have turned their dream apartment into a hell on earth and it is getting worse every week.
- Terrorists are after them. They are blowing up innocent people. They never feel safe and nobody is doing anything about it.
- Their husband has turned out to be a little Peter Pan who takes no responsibility. He won't do the work around the house. He is worse than mother said.

Every problem is blamed on "people," on "flesh and blood." In truth these bothersome people are all mere puppets on a string. The unseen Phantom pulls the strings. This evil enemy is a cunning and mighty adversary. As Martin Luther wrote:

> *For still our ancient foe,*
> *Doth seek to work us woe;*
> *His craft and power are great,*
> *And armed with cruel hate,*
> *On earth is not his equal.*

Armor is essential

If people were only fighting flesh and blood they would not have to live in heavy armor. But against the enemy we are facing it is essential: "Take unto you the whole armor of God" (Ephesians 6:13). The wisest and strongest humans are helpless without Divine armor.

The *Star Wars* warriors used six pieces of armor to protect themselves. Likewise, the Christian warriors who stand against the Dark Prince need six pieces of protection. These provide security in the daily battles and keep them from falling: "Stand therefore, having your loins girt about with truth, and having on the breastplate of righteousness; And your feet shod with the preparation of the gospel of peace; Above all, taking the shield of faith, wherewith you shall be able to quench all the fiery darts of the wicked. And take the helmet of salvation, and the sword of the Spirit, which is the word of God" (Ephesians 6:14-17).

English hymn writer Charles Wesley wrote in response to these verses:

> *Soldiers of Christ, arise,*
> *And put your armor on,*
> *Strong in the strength which God supplies*
> *Through His eternal Son;*
> *Strong in the Lord of hosts,*
> *And in His mighty power,*
> *Who in the strength of Jesus trusts*
> *Is more than conqueror.*

Again Mr. Wesley wrote of man's need for the "whole" armor:

Leave no unguarded place,
No weakness of the soul
Take every virtue, every grace,
And fortify the whole.

1. Protect the waist with a strong belt

Luke always wore a utility "blaster belt." In addition to being of some protection, it held his droid caller, a control box, a chrome pistol and his lightsaber. Han wore the same kind of belt. Princess Leia, the woman of action, uses a symbolic belt worn by Alderaan royalty. The dashing Baron Administrator of Cloud City, Lando Calrissian, protected himself with a wide Baron Administrator state belt. The thick belts on the Imperial Stormtroopers contains blaster power cells, energy rations, and thermal detonators. Chewbacca receives messages on his belt's comlink. The large belt about bounty hunter Boba Fett's waist has a utility pouch.

As a belt protected the fighter's waist in *Star Wars*, the Bible instructs Christians to protect their waists by learning the Bible: "Stand therefore, having your loins girt about with truth" (Ephesians 6:14). And how do we encircle our life with truth? Jesus explained: "Sanctify them through your truth: your word is truth" (John 17:17).

Learning the Bible protects us. The enemy's first attack on Eve was over truth: "Did god say you shall not eat of the fruit of the garden?" But Satan said, "you shall not surely die." If we know the truth Satan cannot deceive us like he did Adam and Eve.

We are secure when we know the truth—God's Word: "Then said Jesus to those Jews which believed on him, If you continue in my word, then are you my disciples indeed; And you shall know the truth, and the truth shall make you free" (John 8:31-32).

2. Secure the chest with a vest

The chest contains the vital organs of humans and the computer parts of droids. In *Star Wars* both humans and droids protected their chests carefully. Luke Skywalker wore a flak vest. The wicked Darth Vader protected his badly injured chest with an armored breast plate. Boba Fett, the mysterious bounty hunter, had an energized blast dissipation vest. Imperial Stormtroopers wore Plastoid composite armor about their chest. General Lando used a metal band about his while posing as a guard at Jabba's palace. Most droids wore decorative metal chest plates, while medical droids were protected by a transparent body shell.

As these soldiers protected the vital organs in their chests with vests, Christians must likewise protect theirs: "Stand therefore...having on the breastplate of righteousness" (Ephesians 6:14). Righteousness means we are cleansed of all our sins and will are not be condemned: "There is therefore now no condemnation for those who are in Christ Jesus" (Romans 8:1). No condemnation! But, if Christians drop this armor and the Devil convinces them they are condemned before God they will fold.

We must always remember these Scriptures and their words of assurance: "Who shall lay any thing to the charge of God's elect? It is God that justifies. Who is he that condemns? It is Christ that died, yea rather, that is risen again, who is even at the right hand of God, who also makes intercession for us. Who shall separate us from the love of Christ?" (Romans 8:33-35). No one can charge a Christian with being unrighteous. Christ died for our sins so we would be made pure before God.

Just as Christ's death makes us righteous before God, His power enables us to live righteously before this world.

"But as many as received him, to them gave he power to become the sons of God" (John 1:12).

When Pharaoh's lovely wife suddenly came on to Joseph, he was ready. He refused her advances. This stirred her anger. She lied and said Joseph had attacked her. So, they put him in prison. Joseph lost his freedom, but not his reputation. His heart was protected from temptation by God's power. Later, he emerged a righteous leader in Egypt.

3. The feet must be protected by proper footwear.

In every army the footwear is crucial for protecting the feet and securing footage in rough country. *Star War's* droids wore magnetic grip foot-plates that enabled their feet to stick to metal surfaces. Luke Skywalker protected his footing with positive grip soles. The strong willed Princess Leia Organa wore travel boots, while the Ice Princess of a lost planet wore military snow boots. The rugged Han Solo wore action boots for his bounty hunting. Reinforced metal foot shells guarded the feet of the protocol droid. Imperial Snowtroopers wore rugged ice boots that enable them to survive for two weeks in deeply frozen country. The elite Imperial pilots used positive gravity pressure boots. The mysterious Boba Fett had spring loaded spikes in the front of his boots.

As soldiers must be protected by proper footwear, Christians must cover their feet with the Gospel of Peace. The Bible says Christians should have their "Feet shod with the preparation of the gospel of peace" (Ephesians 6:15). If a soldier's feet are not well covered he cannot even march, much less fight. For the Christian soldier God's peace is as important as boots to the military.

Dr. Whitby wrote in the *Matthew Henry's Commentary*, that this means: "Be not easily provoked, nor prone to quarrel: but show all gentleness and all long-suffering to all men, and this will certainly preserve you from many great temptations and persecutions"

Scripture promises, "You wilt keep him in perfect peace, whose mind is stayed on you: because he trusteth in you" (Isaiah 26:3). Without God's peace, Satan can stir up family conflicts that wreck the home. But God's peace can protect us when people attack us with criticism, threats, and disrespect.

If Christians are not protected by God's peace bad injuries can be inflicted: Satan can send a wild driver along the highway to provoke them into speeding and having a wreck. A mere argument can end up destroying a wonderful courtship. The boss can aggravate a worker into quitting a good job. Without God's peace, family quarrels can erupt into divorces. Winners must protect their feet with the gospel of peace at all times.

4. The whole person must be protected by a shield

When Darth Vader raises his arms and hurled every loose object at Deak, he protected himself with an invisible shield. Han protected his space ship from an attack by an Imperial cruiser with a deflector shield. Ben trained Luke in the use of a blast shield, despite his complaint he couldn't see. The giant Imperial ship, Death Star, had ray-shields protecting its inner shaft.

The most important of all the armor is the shield. Scripture says, "Above all, taking the shield of faith, wherewith you shall be able to quench all the fiery darts of the wicked" (Ephesians 6:16). Above all else we must constantly keep faith, keep trusting in our Lord for daily victory.

Every man lives by faith. Even the atheist puts his

faith in himself, or something like science. George Bernard Shaw said, "The science to which I pinned my faith is bankrupt. Its counsels, which should have established the millennium, led instead directly to the suicide of Europe. I believed them once. In their name I helped to destroy the faith of millions of worshippers in the temples of a thousand creeds. And now they look at me and witness the great tragedy of an atheist who has lost his faith." Shaw failed to protect himself with the shield of faith in Jesus and he became a casualty.

When Satan fires the fiery darts of persecution that can consume us, faith in Jesus Christ is a protective shield. Peter urged the Christians not to bowled over by the fiery trials of Roman persecution that were about to come upon them. By having faith, in Jesus, they would make it through: "Beloved, think it not strange concerning the fiery trial which is to try you, as though some strange thing happened unto you: But rejoice, inasmuch as you are partakers of Christ's sufferings; that, when his glory shall be revealed, you may be glad also with exceeding joy" (I Peter 4:12-13).

The thing the Apostle Peter was most concerned about was the faith of his followers. He prayed: "That the trial of your faith, being much more precious than of gold that perishes, though it be tried with fire, might be found unto praise and honor and glory at the appearing of Jesus Christ" (I Peter 1:7). Peter knew that through faith they would survive.

The three Hebrew children were carrying the shield of faith when they were ordered to bow to an idol god or be put into a burning oven:

> "Shadrach, Meshach, and Abednego, answered and said to the king, O Nebuchadnezzar, we are not careful to answer you in this matter. If it be so, our God who we serve is able to deliver us from

the burning fiery furnace, and he will deliver us out of your hand, O king. But if not, be it known unto you, O king, that we will not serve your gods, nor worship the golden image which you have set up" (Daniel 3:16-18).

They were protected by the shield of faith and it enabled them to survive the fiery furnace.

5. The head must have the protection of a helmet

Star Wars' righteous warrior, Luke Skywalker, protected his head with an insulated metal helmet bearing the Alliance symbol. Darth Vader covered his misshapen face with a two-part, high-tech, black helmet that had vision enhancement receptors, speech projection, a body heat regulator, an air pump and respiratory vents built in. Droids wore helmets protecting their logic computer system. Stormtrooper officers had reinforced helmets with anti-laser mesh, magnetic shielding, a broadband communications antenna and optical equipment that creates holographic images of the surrounding terrain which enables them to see through smoke, darkness and fire. The Snowtrooper's helmets had breath heaters under their face masks and polarized snow goggles. Imperial pilots had reinforced flight helmets with ship-linked communications built in. Boba Fett, a bounty hunter, wore a helmet which featured a macrobinocular viewplate and a motion/sound sensor system. To top them all, Zuckuss had a helmet with a targeting laser, a ciosion-plus scanner, and a speech scrambler.

Christians are instructed to wear the "the helmet of salvation" (Ephesians 6:17). The head gear is necessary to protect the mind against Satanic fear and worry. Paul wrote: "Now we beseech you, brethren, by the coming of our Lord

Jesus Christ, and by our gathering together unto him, That you be not soon shaken in mind, or be troubled" (II Thessanoians 2:1-2).

The Psalmist wore the helmet of salvation. He explained, "What time I am afraid, I will trust in you" (Psalms 56:3).

Paul's head was always protected from fears about the future by his helmet of salvation: "But let us, who are of the day, be sober, putting on...the hope of salvation. For God has not appointed us to wrath, but to obtain salvation by our Lord Jesus Christ, Who died for us, that, whether we wake or sleep, we should live together with him" (I Thessalonians 5:8-10).

Peter wore the helmet through great trials and temptations: "Blessed be the God and Father of our Lord Jesus Christ, which according to his abundant mercy has begotten us again unto a lively hope by the resurrection of Jesus Christ from the dead, To an inheritance incorruptible, and undefiled, and that fades not away, reserved in heaven for you, Who are kept by the power of God through faith unto salvation ready to be revealed in the last time. Wherein you greatly rejoice, though now for a season, if need be, you are in heaviness through manifold temptations" (I Peter 1:3-6).

We must be protected from all the fears and worries Satan attacks us with. The helmet of salvation does this. It keeps us looking for the victory that is coming: "Looking for that blessed hope, and the glorious appearing of the great God and our Savior Jesus Christ" (Titus 2:13).

6. Enemy assaults must be defended with a sword

In the high-tech world of *Star Wars* the sword was not outdated. But, instead of being made of sharp steel, they flashed deadly laser rays. Darth Maul had a double barrel lightsaber with beams projecting out of each end. Ben Kenobi gave Luke Skywalker his father's light saber. In his hands it burst to life once against and protected him from his Imperial enemies. Laser swords are pure energy blades with no mass. They create powerful electromagnetic arc waves and will detonate if not handled properly. In the classic lightsaber sword fight, Luke and Darth Vader dueled in Cloud City.

The final piece of Christian armor is the Sword of the Spirit: "And take...the sword of the Spirit, which is the word of God" (Ephesians 6:17). The Word is both defensive armor, covering the waist with truth and offensive armor, with which to fight off Satan's attacks: "For the word of God is quick, and powerful, and sharper than any two edged sword, piercing even to the dividing asunder of soul and spirit, and of the joints and marrow, and is a discerner of the thoughts and intents of the heart" (Hebrews 4:12). As the fantasy laserlights cut sharper than swords of steel, so also does the Word of God.

We can become winners by watching Jesus and learning from His example. Every time the Devil confronted Christ in the wilderness, Jesus immediately swung the Sword of the Spirit, God's Word. When the Devil tempted Christ to obey Him and turn the stones to bread, Jesus proclaimed: "It is written, Man shall not live by bread alone, but by every word that proceedeth out of the mouth of God" (Matthew 4:4). Again, when Satan said to jump off the temple and thrill the crowd, Christ swung the sword of Scripture: "It is written again, You shall not tempt the Lord your God" (Matthew 4:7). When Satan begged Christ to bow down and worship him, Jesus countered with the sword: "Then said Jesus unto him, Get you hence, Satan: for it is written, You shall worship the Lord your God, and him only shall you serve" (Matthew

4:10).

Like Jesus, we are protected from the dark Force by depending on the Spirit's power and the Word's cutting Force. Every time the Devil attacks, talk back to him. Quote him Scripture. This will throw back his attacks and make victory certain.

"This armor is not like those antiquated suits we are accustomed to look at in the Tower of London or elsewhere," said Bible commentator E. C. Jennings. "It is for present use, and has never been improved upon. Modern weapons are out of date in a few years—this armor, never. God does not tell us to look at it, to admire it, but to put it on, for amour is of no use until it is put on."

By staying dressed in the mighty armor of God, we can live with security in a scary world.

The massive docking doors cannot hold them.
The magnetically sealed doors fail to contain them.
—*Star Wars*: A New Hope

Chapter 16

BREAKING THROUGH
IMPOSSIBLE BARRIERS

In *Star Wars: A New Hope*, Princess Leia was held inside the Death Star, the prisoner of Darth Vader. Luke and Ben set out to rescue her. But their battered space ship, Millennium Falcon, is caught in a tractor beam and pulled inside the mile-high band of the dreaded Death Star. Stormtroopers awaited their arrival. Huge docking doors seem to seal their fate. But Luke and Han put on stormtrooper uniforms and helmets and start searching for the Princess. They tried to look inconspicuous in their armored suits as they wait for a vacuum elevator to arrive. Troops, bureaucrats, and robots bustle about, ignoring the trio. Luke found Leia . He tells her, "I'm here to rescue you." As they tried to get out a violent laser fight rages inside the evil space ship Death Star. Luke and his fellow freedom fighters were far outnumbered by the Emperor's Troops. They tried to escape the heavy fire of the Imperial Storm Troops by diving into a chute. They landed in the garbage room. Han fired off a laser pistol at the hatch. But it was magnetically sealed and didn't open. Darth Vader learned they were in the garbage room and pressed a button that made the compactor walls close in on them. Just before the good rebels were crushed to death, the power failed and they escaped. Princess Leia, Luke and Han went free. The massive docking doors could not hold them. The magnetically sealed doors fail to contain them.

Hatches, doors and gates were continual challenges to the good Rebels in their war against the Evil Emperor. But these warriors refused to be restrained by the barriers.

Jesus Christ said his followers would face similar barriers—the gates of hell: "I will build my church; and the gates of hell shall not prevail against it" (Matthew 16:18). Christ declared the gates might look impossible but they would not prevail against his soldiers.

Gates are barriers that are put up to confine, restrict, restrain and hinder. They are erected to stop progress, to limit how far we will be able to go. Sometimes we can't see the gates of hell. The Rebels could not see Death Star's protective shield in the *Return of the Jedi* because it was an invisible energy shield.

Ackbar explains, "You can see here the Death Star orbiting the forest moon of En-dor. Although the weapon systems on this Death Star are not yet operational, the Death Star does have a strong defense mechanism. It is protected by an energy shield which is generated from the nearby forest moon of Endor. The shield must be deactivated if any attack is to be attempted. Once the shield is down, our cruisers will create a perimeter, while the fighters fly into the superstructure and attempt to knock out the main reactor. General Calrissian has volunteered to lead the fighter attack." The great breakthrough of the *Star Wars* story came when the Rebels broke through the invisible shield.

Lucifer has erected invisible shields on earth; three energy shields meant to prevent people from reaching their goals—from winning in life. Outside a mass of people are confined by the Devil to a loser's life. Here is how some broke through seemingly impossible barriers.

1. The "wrong person" gate

In *Star Wars: A New Hope,* the stubby astrorobot, Artoo, and his droid friend Threepio were pursued by Vader's stormtroopers. They had just knocked Princess Leia out with rays from a laserpistol. There was an emergency lifepod that might allow them to escape, but the small hatch seems impossible. Also, Threepio warned, "Hey, you're not permitted in there. It's restricted. You'll be deactivated for sure" But Artoo worked his way past the hatch door and was joined by Threepio. They blasted off and escape the stormtroopers just in time. The two unlikely creatures lack human intelligence. They are slow and clumsy. But they escaped to play an important role in the war with the Empire.

There is a passage through which many might escape were it not for the, "wrong person" gate. The sign on this gate reads, "You are inferior. You can never get by this." Like a massive mirror, this gate reflects every weakness, every inadequacy, every shortcoming of those who approach it. This gate is invisible. We cannot touch it or even see it. It exists in the minds of people. But it effectively keeps many people from winning.

Moses, the man who would be known as the great liberator of the Jewish people, spent most of his life confined by

this gate. God called him to set the children of Israel free— to liberate them from the harsh bondage of Egypt's Pharaoh.

Standing before the "wrong person," Moses "said unto God, Who am I, that I should go unto Pharaoh, and that I should bring forth the children of Israel out of Egypt?... Behold, they will not believe me, nor hearken unto my voice" (Exodus 3:11, 4:1). "And Moses said unto the LORD, O my Lord, I am not eloquent...I am slow of speech, and of a slow tongue. And the LORD said unto him, Who has made man's mouth? or who makes the dumb, or deaf, or the seeing, or the blind? have not I the LORD? Now therefore go, and I will be with your mouth, and teach you what you shall say. And he said, O my Lord, send, I pray you, by the hand of him who you wilt send" (Exodus 4:10-13).

Moses said, in effect, "Lord I have great faith that you can do it, but not with me. Get someone else. Get Aaron."

The Jewish people had to wait until Moses was 80-years-old before he had enough faith to crash this gate and lead his people to freedom. But he did, and he proved that the gates of hell will not prevail, not even against a stuttering, inferior, old man.

To encourage those held captive behind this invisible gate, God has given an aptitude test. It says: "God has chosen the foolish things of the world to confound the wise; and God has chosen the weak things of the world to confound the things which are mighty; And base things of the world, and things which are despised, has God chosen, yea, and things which are not, to bring to nothing things that are: That no flesh should glory in his presence" (I Corinthians 1:27-29).

This passage raises five simple questions to tell how qualified we are to do heroic things on the battlefield of life.

1   Are we wise? If so, we might be able to do

something, but we will be handicapped because we will trust in our own wisdom instead
of God's. Jehovah is looking for the foolish,
who have to trust His wisdom.

2 Are we strong? If we are, we will be limited in
service by trusting our strength instead of
God's.

3 Are we base, low-class people? If so our reputation will not detract from building the reputation of the Lord.

4 Are we despised by others? God uses people
who seek to build a reputation in Heaven at the
price of being disliked on earth.

5 Are we just absolutely nothing? God selects
those who are the world's "nothings."

If we are foolish, weak, low down, despised nothings,
we score 100 on this aptitude test for God's service. We are
just the people God is looking for to be gate crashers.

Norman Grubb said, "Faith is not believing God is
almighty. Faith is believing God is almighty in you. Faith is
not believing God can do anything. Faith is believing God can
do anything through you." Faith believes that the gates of hell
cannot prevail, regardless of our limitations.

The Bible invites us to just look about us and see who
God is using: "For you see your calling, brethren, how that
not many wise men after the flesh, not many mighty, not many
noble, are called" (I Corinthians 1:26).

A man in Jacksonville, Florida became a Christian but
would not go to church for a year because he was afraid he
would be embarrassed. He couldn't read and he knew the
singer would say, "turn to hymn number 15 and let's sing."
Then the preacher would say, "turn to Matthew chapter five

and read with me." Finally, after a year, he got up enough courage to start attending the First Baptist Church of Jacksonville. One day the pastor, Dr. Homer Lindsay, Jr. wisely told his congregation, "Everybody can do something important for the Lord. I have some tracts down here. If you can't do anything else, you can pass them out and show people how to become Christians. He thought, "you don't have to be able to read to do that. I could give out tracts."

The man developed a strange approach. He would walk up to busy men on the sidewalks of Jacksonville and say, "Pardon me sir. I can't read. I wonder if you would read this for me." Of course, the man would read the tract and then he would say, "I can't read it but I sure can explain it. Let me tell you what this means." Using this unique approach he led 30 people to become Christians and walk down the aisle of the First Baptist Church to confirm their decision in one year!

I told Dr. Lindsay, "Don't ever let him learn how to read. He would be as dead as the rest of us."

2. The "wrong place" gate

Aboard the ship Death Star, Luke and Leia were stranded on a perilous perch. There was a hatch door in front of them, but it was shut. Blast from the stormtrooper's laser weapons were exploding around them. Every way of escape was closed. It appeared the hatch would not open. Luke and Leia were in a place that offered no hope. In another situation they might have made it, but not there. Yet, Luke didn't give up. He pulled a thin nylon cable from his trooper utility belt with a grappler hook on it. Luke threw it across a gorge and the trapped pair swung to safety.

Satan's second gate is the "wrong place" gate. On it there is a bold sign declaring, "You can't win here. Maybe somewhere else, but not here." It tells men God can do great things, he might be able to do these with them, but not where they are. The Devil calls every place a hard, difficult, impossible one.

This was the gate that stared Jesus' disciples in the face. Christ told them, "That repentance and remission of sins should be preached in his name among all nations, beginning at Jerusalem" (Luke 24:47).

Jerusalem? Why, this is the city that had killed the prophets! Jerusalem! This is the city that had just killed Jesus! Jerusalem had to be the hardest place on earth. Yet, Jesus commanded, "beginning at Jerusalem."

In Jerusalem God's power came on frail weak men. They saw 3,000 converted from the Devil's side to God's side. Then they saw 5,000 converted. There was no stopping them: "And the word of God increased; and the number of the disciples multiplied in Jerusalem greatly; and a great company of the priests were obedient to the faith" (Acts 6:7).

God wanted to settle this for all ages. If He can do it with this frail, foolish group in Jerusalem, the hardest place on earth, He can do it anywhere on this planet. A person's place may be hard, but it is not too hard.

When Mao took over in China, he was determine to win a great victory for the Devil. He vowed to destroy Christianity. Mao closed all the churches, shipped out all the missionaries, imprisoned all the ministers and burned all the Bibles he could find. Today, Mao is dead and gone. But Christians have grown from one million to fifty million believers. China was the "hardest place" on earth, but these gate crashers won the victory right there, where they were. They won in spite of being in a hopeless situation.

3. The "wrong time" gate

Han and Chewbacca were running down a corridor on

Death Star exchanging laser fire with several troopers in close pursuit. Suddenly, large blast doors began to close in front of them. It seemed they were too late. They had missed their opportunity. Perhaps later the doors would open and they would have a chance. But the young starpilot and his furry friend seized the moment and dashed through just in the nick of time. Those heavy blast doors did not prevail.

Satan's third gate is the "wrong time" gate. There is a sign painted on it that says, "Not now. This is not the right time. You cannot do it now. Maybe later."

While the gate says "later," God says now! "Behold, now is the accepted time; behold, now is the day of salvation" (II Corinthians 6:2). The winners are those who refuse to wait and crash the gates like the *Star Wars* heroes.

The Bible tells the story of an immoral woman who got saved and refused to stay behind the "not now" gate. She crashed through it to a fantastic victory:

> Then comes he (Jesus) to a city of Samaria, which is called Sychar, near to the parcel of ground that Jacob gave to his son Joseph. Now Jacob's well was there. Jesus therefore, being wearied with his journey, sat thus on the well: and it was about the sixth hour. There comes a woman of Samaria to draw water: Jesus said unto her, Give me to drink....Then said the woman of Samaria unto him, How is it that you, being a Jew, askest drink of me, which am a woman of Samaria? for the Jews have no dealings with the Samaritans. Jesus answered and said unto her, If you knew the gift of God, and who it is that said to you, Give me to drink; you would have asked of him, and he would have given you living water. The woman

said unto him, Sir, you have nothing to draw with, and the well is deep: from whence then have you that living water? Art you greater than our father Jacob, which gave us the well, and drank thereof himself, and his children, and his cattle? Jesus answered and said unto her, Whosoever drinks of this water shall thirst again: But whosoever drinks of the water that I shall give him shall never thirst; but the water that I shall give him shall be in him a well of water springing up into everlasting life. The woman said unto him, Sir, give me this water, that I thirst not, neither come hither to draw. Jesus said unto her, Go, call your husband, and come hither. The woman answered and said, I have no husband. Jesus said unto her, You have well said, I have no husband: For you have had five husbands; and he who you now have is not your husband: in that said you truly. The woman said unto him, Sir, I perceive that you art a prophet. Our fathers worshipped in this mountain; and you say, that in Jerusalem is the place where men ought to worship Jesus said unto her, Woman, believe me, the hour comes, when you shall neither in this mountain, nor yet at Jerusalem, worship the Father. You worship you know not what: we know what we worship: for salvation is of the Jews. But the hour comes, and now is, when the true worshippers shall worship the Father in spirit and in truth: for the Father seek such to worship him. God is a Spirit: and they that worship him must worship him in spirit and in truth. The woman said unto him, I know that Messiah comes, which is called Christ: when he is come, he will tell us all things.

Jesus said unto her, I that speak unto you am he. And upon this came his disciples, and marveled that he talked with the woman: yet no man said, What seek you? or, Why talk you with her? The woman then left her waterpot, and went her way into the city, and said to the men, Come, see a man, which told me all things that ever I did: is not this the Christ? Then they went out of the city, and came unto him....And many of the Samaritans of that city believed on him for the saying of the woman, which testified, He told me all that ever I did. So when the Samaritans were come unto him, they besought him that he would tarry with them: and he abode there two days. And many more believed because of his own word; And said unto the woman, Now we believe, not because of your saying: for we have heard him ourselves, and know that this is indeed the Christ, the Savior of the world (John 4:5-42).

This woman gave a heroic example for all the following ages. She did what Jesus said to do: "Say not you, There are yet four months, and then comes harvest? behold, I say unto you, Lift up your eyes, and look on the fields; for they are white already to harvest" (John 4:35).

The lowly Samaritan crashed the gates of hell and liberated a city of humans bound by the dark Force. She made it through the "this is not the right time gate." She didn't put it off until she had studied, gotten better prepared, and had more experience. She did it immediately without waiting to study, getting better prepared, or more experienced. This great gate crasher set a whole city free the first day she came to know Jesus!

Christ said, "And from the days of John the Baptist until now the kingdom of heaven suffers violence, and the violent take it by force" (Matthew 11:12). The Kingdom of Heaven is for the desperate. It is for aggressive people like Luke and Han who will not be denied, for men who are fanatically earnest, and for men who believe the gates of hell will not prevail against them.

Paul McGuire, a Christian writer, said, "Jesus clearly says that the church should be like a great heavenly battering ram smashing down the gates of hell and freeing the captive inside."[39]

Everyone being limited in life, everyone who seems unable to reach their goal, and everyone discouraged by the gates of hell, should claim Christ's promise that the gates of hell would not prevail.

Consider these three question raised by Paul Harvey:

> *If not us, who?*
> *If not here, where?*
> *If not now, when?*

*Death Star's commander, Moff Jerierrod, a tall, confident
technocrat, and Darth Vader, Lord of the Sith, kneeled in
the presence of the Emperor. The Supreme Ruler of the galaxy slowly makes his way before a row of troops. They
kneel along with their commanders. He is the supreme
ruler of the dark Force. He is an evil god.*
—Return of the Jedi

Chapter 17
THE DARK FORCE
TAKES A HUMAN FORM

Evil becomes most dangerous when it takes a human form.
In *Episode I* the dark Force took the human body of Darth
Maul, Dark Lord of Sith, to do his evil work in. In *Star
Wars Episode VI*, evil took the form of an Emperor, the Supreme Ruler of the Galactic Empire and Master of the dark
side of the Force. This Emperor used his great power to
bring suffering and death to all who refused to bow before
him. He was merciless. Even Darth Vader, a vicious man
himself, told a commander, "The Emperor is not as forgiving as I am."

Just like the Emperor in the *Star Wars* fantasy, the
Bible says evil will one day be embodied in a human form.

The Phantom Prince will one day tire of being without due recognition even though he is "the god of this world." Then he will take on a human body and become the recognized ruler of the earth. For one glorious, fleeting moment the dark Force will reach the height of his evil career as the human Antichrist.

No one recognizes
the man of sin

The Emperor is a deceiver. He fools Luke Sky-walker into believing he has no weapon, but pulls a sword out of his sleeve. People do not realize how evil the *Star Wars* Emperor is. Only after Luke is taken prisoner by the Supreme Ruler in *The Return of the Jedi* does he get a close look into his eyes. Then he realizes just how evil the Emperor is. Likewise, the Antichrist will deceive people. They will think he is a good leader, a wonderful Messiah who will save them, when he really is the most wicked figure in history. He "Deceives them that dwell on the earth" (Revelation 13:14). The enemy of Christ will: "Be a deceiver...an Antichrist" (II John 1:7). The whole world will be fooled for he "Deceives the whole world" (Revelation 12:9).

The reason people will be tricked is they have not loved the truth—they have not read and studied their Bibles: "Even him, whose coming is after the working of Satan with all power and signs and lying wonders, And with all deceivableness of unrighteousness in them that perish; because they received not the love of the truth, that they might be saved" (II Thessalonians 2:9-10). Had they studied Scripture they would have recognized Satan.

The mysterious talking image

The Galactic Emperor had the power to project a lifelike, talking, holographic image of himself. In the communication chamber his image appeared to Jer-jerrod. He knelt before that image and listened as it commanded him to bring Luke Skywalker to him. On another occasion, a twelve-foot hologram of the Galactic Emperor materializes before Darth Vader.

As in the *Star Wars*, the Antichrist will command humans to make him a lifelike image: "Saying to them that dwell on the earth, that they should make an image to the beast" (Revelation 13:14). The Antichrist will give it the power of life. He will speak through it and demand that men bow down and worship his image: "And he had power to give life unto the image of the beast, that the image of the beast should both speak" (Revelation 13:15).

A commanding voice

Dark Vader had a thundering voice, but the Emperor's voice was even deeper and more frightening. The ruler's mighty voice helped him control his empire.

The Antichrist will, likewise, move the masses with his voice. The Bible says he will have: "A mouth speaking great things" (Daniel 7:8). Again the Bible says: "And there was given unto him a mouth speaking great things" (Revelation 13:5). In addition to superior speaking ability, he will be superior in looks: "a mouth that spoke very great things, whose look was more stout than his fellows" (Daniel 7:20).

The Antichrist will be just right for a world of satel-

lites and worldwide television. His ability to communicate will enable him to sway the masses. Character will no longer matter. The Antichrist's appearance and voice will sway the masses. People will think he is the greatest person on earth, saying, "Who is like him" (Revelation 13:4). It is said that he "will combine the logic of a Churchill, the emotion of a Hitler, and the wit of a Kennedy."

The rise of a worldwide empire

The commanders of the universe bow when the Master of the Universe passes by. All the creatures in the universe submit to his rule except for a small group of Rebels. In *The Empire Strikes Back*, his most dreaded battle station has been destroyed. The Emperor shows his political power by declaring martial law throughout the galaxy. A million planets felt the Imperial grip of the Emperor's stormtroopers. With the tightening of the Emperor's oppression, only a small group of Rebels were not under his control, and these were searching for a safe place to hide.

In the last days the Antichrist will have this kind of rule over the world: "Power was given him over all kindreds, and tongues, and nations. And all that dwell upon the earth...whose names are not written in the book of life of the Lamb slain from the foundation of the world" (Revelation 13:7-8). Everyone will bow to this last day Caesar except true Christians who will rebel.

The evil Phantom's rise to worldwide power will begin in a new Roman Empire. It will be the fourth and last of the great Gentile powers. The first world power was Babylon, pictured by a lion with eagle's wings" (Daniel

7:4). The second was the great Media-Persian Empire, pictured by a bear: "a second, like to a bear" (Daniel 7:5). The third world power was the Greek Empire, pictured by a leopard: "And lo another, like a leopard" (Daniel 7:6).

The fourth empire was the Roman Empire, pictured by a dreadful beast: "After this I saw in the night visions, and behold a fourth beast, dreadful and terrible, and strong exceedingly" (Daniel 7:7). This beast is made of strong iron, like the mighty Roman Empire. It will have, on its extreme end, two feet, describing the Roman Empire which was divided into two parts. At the extreme end of the image were the ten toes. These represent the ten countries that will unite at the extreme end of history: "And whereas you saw the feet and toes, part of potters' clay, and part of iron, the kingdom shall be divided; but there shall be in it of the strength of the iron, forasmuch as you saw the iron mixed with miry clay. And as the toes of the feet were part of iron, and part of clay, so the kingdom shall be partly strong, and partly broken" (Daniel 2:41-42).

After the Antichrist gains control of the old Roman Empire, he will expand his rule over the whole world. Under the Antichrist's rule, this empire will be expanded until it encompasses the world: "devour the whole earth."

As Darth Vader stood with his back turned, his uncovered head was exposed. A droid attends him. A respirator tube now retracts from Vader's head. Without his black helmet a mass of ugly scar tissue can be seen. It covers his large head. Before the droid lowers his mask and helmet onto Vader, we realize he has survived a terrible head blow.

Like Darth Vader, the Antichrist will receive a severe head wound. The Antichrist will stun the world by re-

covering from an apparently fatal head wound: "The beast, which had the wound by a sword, and did live" (Revelation 13:14). Again, the Bible says: "And I saw one of his heads as it were wounded to death; and his deadly wound was healed: and all the world wondered after the beast" (Revelation 13:3). This will help his rise to power. Imagine what would have happened if President John F. Kennedy had recovered from the fatal wound in Dallas.

The Antichrist shall rise to power on a platform of peace and prosperity. Step by step he moves up to become the leader of the entire world. To unify the world the Antichrist will have to overcome nationalism. God created separate nations at the Tower of Babel by dividing the languages of people. The purpose was the same as that of the framers of the United States Constitution; to prevent any man or group from abusing power. Satan fought a long uphill battle against the strong spirit of nationalism.

The "peace and prosperity" platform
Today, two forces are working in the Devil's favor. People want a world-wide financial union so they can make more money. Also, they want someone to control all nations and keep them from starting wars. The Antichrist will unify people by promising them what they want—peace and prosperity (Daniel 8:25, 11:24).

This future world ruler will have so much power he can change long standing laws and even the way the world has recorded time: "And he shall...think to change times and laws: and they shall be given into his hand until a time and times and the dividing of time" (Daniel 7:25).

The Christian era began with a world government ruled by one man—Caesar—who was obeyed as king and worshipped as god. The Christian era will end the same way with a world government ruled by a last days Caesar who will be obeyed as king and worshipped as god.

Arnold Toynbee, the eminent historian, said on a radio broadcast that "By forcing on mankind more and more lethal weapons, and at the same time making the world more and more interdependent economically, technology has brought mankind to such a degree of distress that we are ripe for the deifying of any new Caesar who might succeed in giving the world unity and peace."

A beast controls
the money

The well disguised Phantom will fulfill his pledge of economic prosperity, causing "craft to prosper" to prosper in the land: "He shall cause craft to prosper in his land" (Daniel 8:25). Prosperity will rain like water. Everyone is thrilled. No one cares what the Antichrist does. He is the hero of a world that measures leaders by the success of the economy.

Then he will move swiftly to gain complete control of the world's money supply. The time has been coming for many years. There is a growing discontent with the nation's money system. Back in 1973 *U. S. News & World Report* declared , "In Sight Now: A New World Money Plan."[40] The European Union took a bold step by introducing the "Euro." Computers have made it possible to handle money matters electronically. International banking and fund transfers have been made possible by satellites. People have been preparing for a cashless society for decades:

Tiny computer chips are being implanted in animals for proper identification, health records,and to prevent theft. Chips can easily and safely be implanted in humans. Suppose we did this. It could end tax fraud, illegal drug,and trafficking. One day the Antichrist will use some similar technology to control human buying and selling: "And that no man might buy or sell, save he that had the mark, or the name of the beast, or the number of his name" (Revelation 13:17).

The brilliance of this scheme is astonishing. An unsuspecting world will enable the entire money supply of the whole world to be controlled by one man.

I was renting a car in Memphis, Tennessee when a business man came charging toward the counter. He wasn't just another guy in a hurry; he appeared desperate.

"Young lady, my plane was late; I'm about to miss a very, very important meeting; I've got to have a car right away. Could you rent me one in a hurry?" The young lady asked for his credit card and ran it through the little computer scanner. It was maxed out. Likewise, the computer rejected a second and a third card. They too had reached their limits. The man pulled out a roll of money and said, "I'll pay you cash." She replied, "Sir, I'm sorry, but our company does not allow me to rent cars without a valid credit card."

As the man walked away chills went down my spine. I thought, somewhere in a little room, a man with a computer had typed in the command that when this man's card reached a certain maximum he could no longer buy with it. I thought, someday a single man with a computer will be able to type in a command to cancel any man's number and in a cashless society he would not even be able to buy a loaf of bread.

A man will be
worshipped as god

In the *Return of the Jedi*, The Emperor arrived on the half-completed Death Star. When he stepped out Darth Vader and thousands of Imperial troops awaited him in the docking bay. The Emperor's Royal Guard proceeded with him down the corridor and created a security zone. Then the Emperor slowly made his way down the ramp. Death Star's commander, Moff Jerierrod, a tall, confident technocrat, and Darth Vader, Lord of the Sith, knelt in the presence of the Emperor. The Supreme Ruler of the galaxy slowly made his way before a row of troops. They knelt along with their commanders. He was the supreme ruler of the dark Force. He was a god.

The coming Antichrist will demand that men bow before him and worship him: "Let no man deceive you by any means: for that day shall not come, except there come a falling away first, and that man of sin be revealed, the son of perdition; Who opposes and exalts himself above all that is called God, or that is worshipped; so that he as God sits in the temple of God, shewing himself that he is God" (II Thessalonians 2:3-4).

Everyone except Christians will bow to the Antichrist: "And all that dwell upon the earth shall worship him, whose names are not written in the book of life of the Lamb slain from the foundation of the world" (Revelation 13:8).

Only those who bow and worship the Antichrist will retain the number embedded in their bodies making it possible for them to buy bread and live: "If any man worship the beast and his image, and receive his mark in his forehead, or in his hand" (Revelation 14:9).

Demanding worship should not be surprising from this last Caesar. The first temple the Caesars built for people to worship them in was erected to the godhead of the Emperor in Pergamum in 29 B.C. In that year Caesar worship began. The vast Empire of Rome was brought together by a common religion. Soon every Roman citizen was crying, "Caesar is Lord." The Antichrist will continue the tradition.

Lucifer has been working from before the fall from Heaven to be worshipped like God. For a short time he will achieve this while he is in the body of the Antichrist.

He rules with brutal military might

Darth Vader, the evil prince of *Star Wars*, was feared throughout the universe because of his great power. But Lawrence Kasdan said, "My sense of the relationship is that the Emperor is much more powerful than Vader and that Vader is very much intimidated by him. Vader has dignity, but the Emperor...really has all the power." The Emperor commanded much more deadly power than Vader.

The ruler of the Empire possesses supernatural powers within his body. The Emperor can raise his hand and cause the powerful Vader to start choking helplessly. The Galactic ruler sends lightning bolts flying from his fingers to strike Luke. These blinding bolts of lightning blast from the Emperor's hands knock out Ben. They flash at Luke with such speed the young Jedi is knocked to the ground. The Emperor stands over Luke as he lay on the floor writhing in pain. He says, "Young fool.., only now, at the end, do you understand. Your feeble skills are no match for the power of the dark side."

The powers of the Emperor's dark side include an army of deadly stormtroopers, a fleet of mighty space ships, and Death Star, a ship that can blow planets into dust with one laser beam. When the Emperor appears in public, thousands of Imperial troops in tight formation protect him. This was demonstrated at the mammoth docking bay of Death Star.

Like the fantasy Emperor, the Antichrist will have supreme power. Humans throughout the world will say, "Who is able to make war with him?" (Revelation 13:4) His tremendous military might will scare the world into submission.

Revelation 13:2 takes us on a trip to the zoo to explain how terrifying the Antichrist's power will be: "And the beast which I saw was like a leopard, and his feet were like those of a bear, and his mouth like the mouth of a lion." As a speedy leopard quickly seizes his prey, this future ruler will move swiftly against his enemies. Like a powerful bear, the Antichrist will be a mighty killer. And, as the regal lion he will rule with deadly confidence.

Everyone will worship him, except true Christians, will see this as an abandonment of their faith and an act of idolatry. As a result they will be subjected to horrible persecution and in the end to martyrdom. Such will the power of the Antichrist be. Either worship him or die.

"I beheld, and the same horn made war with the saints, and prevailed against them" (Daniel 7:21). In the Revelation of the future, the Bible says, "And it was given unto him to make war with the saints, and to overcome them" (Revelation 13:7).

War drums echo through the universe.
They are calling forth the Empire's
unstoppable war machine. The thunder
of death echoes through the universe.
The Emperor's mighty military force is unleashed.

Chapter 18

A WORLD BATHES IN BLOOD

History climaxes in war. *Star Wars: Episode I—The Phantom Menace* began in a period of civil warfare during the 33rd Century. This episode erupts into a battle between 8,000 droids and Gungan warriors in the final battle scene.

In the final movie, *Episode VI—Return of the Jedi*, the story climaxed in the greatest of all wars. A million stars shuddered at the impact of the fighting. Never before has there been a conflict like it. And never will there be another. The largest planet man has made, Death Star, is ravaged by the slaughter. It is the bloodiest conflict in the history of the Galactic Kingdom.

Star Wars' Princess Leia went through a war that all but wiped out her species. But there was *A New Hope*. The

Rebels of the good Force won a battle against the Empire of the dark Force. The planet-destroying ship, Death Star, was itself destroyed.

But then, in the *Empire Strikes Back*, the Imperial troops pursued the Rebels across the galaxy. Darth Vader dispatches a thousand probes into the outer reaches of space to find Luke. The fighting continues. Luke is wounded. It is a dark time for the Rebels. But, in the *Return of the Jedi*, Luke leads his forces back and the crucial battle between good and evil unfolds.

And from the vivid world of illusion comes a prophecy of what lies ahead for the planet earth—Armageddon. Lucifer will fulfill his great desire to be worshipped as god in the person of the Antichrist. But he has another passion, a greater passion, that must be satisfied. Jesus said, "He was a murderer from the beginning." He loves killing. He loves war. Finally, he shall lose this passion in a killing rampage that will bathe the world in blood.

Lulling the world to sleep

At the beginning of the *Star Wars* film, *Return of the Jedi*, the Galactic Empire is secretly building a new Death Star ship which is even more powerful than the first ship destroyed in *A New Hope*. The Rebels do not suspect anything. Luke and the good Rebels have no idea that their enemies are building the ultimate weapon. While they look for a time of peace, war is on the way. Little do they know that the evil Emperor will soon have the power to rain death throughout the universe. Doom is approaching for the Rebels, and they and expect a thing.

Like the dark Force in *Star Wars*, the Devil will convince the world that there will be peace on earth. Mankind must be lulled to sleep. Earth's dominant superpowers must focus on arms reductions, troop down-sizing, and peace agreements. Around the world an unsuspecting cry will be heard, "Peace, peace." It will sound like the days of Judah's deceptive leaders when the people cried, "Peace, peace; when there is no peace" (Jeremiah 6:14, 8:11).

Then the stage will be set for a reign of terror. The evil Phantom will launch an opening attack on the Jews. They are the people who brought Jesus into the world and the Devil wants them dead. Hitler's plan of extermination of the Jewish race will be brought back.

The Jews will be caught off guard. They will be depending on a "covenant"— a peace treaty with their enemies. The Antichrist will participate in a treaty that will promise seven years of peace in Israel: "He shall confirm the covenant" (Daniel 9:27) They will be allowed to rebuild their temple. Once again they will worship and offer their sacrifices to Jehovah.

But after three and one-half years of peace under the Antichrist's reign, the covenant will be broken. The Antichrist will turn upon the unsuspecting Jews. "He shall cause the sacrifice and the oblation to cease, and...he shall make it desolate" (Daniel 9:27).

A reign of destruction shall begin that will be far worse than all the past atrocities and wars these persecuted people have suffered: "Then shall be great tribulation, such as was not since the beginning of the world to this time, no, nor ever shall be. And except those days should be shortened, there should no flesh be saved" (Matthew 24:21-22).

For three and one-half years war will devastate Israel. They will learn in war what God had tried to teach them in peace, that treaties with the Devil are no good. God said, "Because you have said, We have made a covenant with death, and with hell are we at agreement; when the overflow-

ing scourge shall pass through, it shall not come unto us: for
we have made lies our refuge, and under falsehood have we
hid ourselves:...Your covenant with death shall be disan-
nulled, and your agreement with hell shall not stand; when the
overflowing scourge shall pass through, then you shall be
trodden down by it" (Isaiah 28:15, 18).

During the *Star Wars*, attacks came against the Rebels from three directions: the north, the south and the east. It
will be the same in earth's coming conflict.

An attack from the north

In the Empire Strikes back, the Rebels are very confident. Dack tells Luke, "Right now I feel like I could take on
the whole Empire myself. Luke agrees. Then a Rebel officer
looks across the bleak landscape through his dec-
trobinoculars. He zooms in on two dot-size objects just appearing on the horizon. They are coming closer. He recognizes them as giant Imperial snowwalkers. More appear. An
alarm sounds. Pilots and gunners rush to their snowspeeders.
A trench officer announces he has spotted the Imperial soldiers. A controller echoes the alarm, "Imperial walkers on the
north ridge." The Rebel troops brace for the attack from their
north.

In our present world the dark Force will send a
mighty army from the north against the Jews: "And at the
time of the end shall...the king of the north shall come against
him like a whirlwind, with chariots, and with horsemen, and
with many ships" (Daniel 11:40). Russia and her allies will
launch a massive land and sea attack on the outnumbered
Jewish people.

Ezekiel describe this attack: "And the word of the
Lord came unto me, saying, "Son of man, set your face
against Gog, the land of Magog...In that day when my people

of Israel dwell safely, shall you not know it? And you shall come from your place out of the north parts, you, and many people with you...and you shall come up against my people of Israel, as a cloud to cover the land; it shall be in the latter days" (Ezekiel 38:1-2, 14-16).

Magog is an ancient name for the land we call Russia. Josephus, the respected ancient historian, said the descendants of Noah's grandson Magog were the Scythians who migrated north to the land between the Caspian and Black Seas. He said, "The Scythians were called Magog or Magogites, by the Greeks."[41] The identification of Russia is made unmistakable by the phrase "from the north," which means, in Hebrew, the "uttermost part of the north." The "most northern" country above Israel has to be Russia.

The Devil will bait Russian into this war by presenting an opportunity to seize riches: "And you shall say; I will go to them that are at rest, that dwell safely, all of them dwelling without walls, and having neither bars nor gates. To take a spoil and to take a prey" (Ezekiel 38:11-12).

This will prove to be a great disaster for the northern army. One-sixth of the great Russian forces will die on the mountains of Israel: "And I will turn you back, and leave but the sixth part of you, and will cause you to come up from the north parts, and will bring you upon the mountains of Israel" (Ezekiel 39:2).

A southern attack

The *Star Wars* Rebels were attacked from the south by Imperial walkers. They fired lasers that knock down a gun tower. They hit Zev's snowspeeder with a laserbolt and the cockpit explodes in a ball of flame. The Rebel command center is hit. The walls crack. Pipes break, sending steam billowing through the underground hallways. Leia, who is on one of

the control boards, shouts, "Send all troops in sector twelve to the south slope to protect the fighters."

Israel will also be attacked from the south. The prophet Daniel wrote "And at the time of the end shall the king of the south push at him" (Daniel 11:40). From the first to the last book of the Bible "king of the south" never refers to but one country; the ancient enemy of the Jews—Egypt.

While the Devil deceives Egypt into thinking she is going to gain vengeance against Israel, she will find nothing but death. The nation of Egypt and her Jew-hating allies will be destroyed: "The sword shall come upon Egypt, and great pain shall be in Ethiopia, when the slain shall fall in Egypt... Ethiopia and Libya and Lydia and all the mingled people, and Chub, and the men of the land that is in league, shall fall with them by the sword" (Ezekiel 30:4-5).

Four thousand years ago, on the night of the Jewish Passover, a war began between the Egyptians and the Jews that will climax with this nation from the south invading Israel. A wicked Pharaoh made slaves out of the Jews in Egypt. After years of persecution Moses led their escape from bondage to their home in Israel. This escape was made possible after the eldest son in every Egyptian home died on the night of the Passover. An angry Pharaoh and his army pursued the fleeing Jews and were drown in the Red Sea.

All the centuries that have past have failed to cool the wild hatred between the Egyptians and the Jews. The Antichrist will one day fan this fury to the point that Egypt will attack Israel.

An attack from the East

In *Star Wars*, Luke Skywalker is knocked out and carried off by the Sand People who came from the east. Threepio had given the warning that these fierce creatures

were approaching from the southeast. When one of the tower-
ing creatures swung his dreaded double-pointed ax blades at
him, Luke managed to block the blow with his laser rifle. But
the rifle is smashed and Luke is knocked out by the sinister
Raider and dropped in a heap.

Later, another attack comes from the east. A Rebel
force is fighting in Cloud City. As they try to escape, the evil
Darth Vader appears at the east bay landing platform. They
lock in combat. Their swords collide and the platform beneath
them wavers at the fighting.

Just as in *Star Wars*, a third attack will come against
Israel from the East. The water of the Euphrates will dry up
for the armies to cross and attack Israel: "The sixth angel
poured out his vial upon the great river Euphrates; and the
water thereof was dried up, that the way of the kings of the
east might be prepared" (Revelation 16:12).

The Euphrates River is strategic in world history. It
flows through the cradle of the world's civilization. It has
served as the border of the Garden of Eden, the land of Abraham and the Roman Empire. Creation's first birth and its first
murder took place here in Eden. In defiance of God Himself,
the tower of Babel was erected near the Euphrates. Nimrod
built Babylon, one of the great wonders of the world, on its
ancient river banks. Twenty-one Bible references make it the
most prominent river in prophecy.

In 1976 Arabs, using Russian money, completed a dam
across the Euphrates River forming Lake Assad in Turkey.
Since then, drying up the river Euphrates is as simple as
pressing a button and closing the dam.

Following Iraq's invasion of Kuwait, a retired U. S.
army general was asked about the possibility of poisoning the
Euphrates, devastating the Iraq's main source of fresh water.
The general was emphatic, "No! That is not the thing to do.

We should just dry it up," So what was prophesied in the Bible nearly 2000 yeas ago is, today, a viable military option. Someday the Euphrates will be shutoff to make way for the killers from the East.

The army that will cross the Euphrates will be huge, numbering 200 million: "The number of the army of the horsemen were two hundred thousand thousand: and I heard the number of them." The book of Revelation declares, "And the sixth angel sounded, and I heard a voice from the four horns of the golden altar which is before God, saying to the sixth angel who had the trumpet. Loose the four angels who are bound in the great river Euphrates. And the four angels were loosed, who were prepared for an hour, and a day, and a month, and a year, to slay the third part of men" (Revelation 9:13-15).

Two hundred million soldiers was an impossible figure when John wrote this. Perhaps this is why John said, "I heard the number of them," It was as if someone was questioning him, looking over the disciple's shoulder and saying, "Wait, John, you must have made a miscalculation. You describe an army of 200 million troops and there aren't that many people on earth." The world's population is estimated to have been near 180 million at the time.

John responded to such disbelief when he wrote, "I heard the number of them." As John saw it, he was simply a secretary writing down what God Himself dictated. Late in the 20th Century, Red China's population exploded to over 1.2 billion people and for the first time the world saw a nation capable of fielding an army of 200 million.

In a great blunder, the United States State Department neglected the "king of the East." At the end of World War II the attitude was, "forget the East." Americans thought China and the other countries of the Far East were too far behind to ever be a factor in the Atomic Age.

But there were voices warning us. The man who graduated from West Point Military Academy with the highest academic average of anyone ever graduating from that establishment, a man who read his Bible daily, and a man who was one of the greatest American experts on the Far East, General Douglas MacArthur, said at the end of World War II, "Send me 50,000 missionaries and I will save you sending your boys back to the East to fight." We didn't send the missionaries and we went back to fight in Korea, Cambodia, and Vietnam.

In his historic V-J Day address, delivered from Tokyo Bay, General Douglas MacArthur said, "We have had our last chance. If we do not devise some more greater and equitable system, Armageddon will be at our door." History tell us America missed that chance. Entering the 21st Century North Korea has missiles that can reach American soil and China has become a nuclear power.

Napoleon Bonaparte advised, "Let China sleep, for when China awakes let the nations tremble." China has awakened and is giving the world good cause to tremble. Her gigantic population and vast military capabilities make her a deadly military threat.

Napoleon advised us well about letting China sleep. Now the power of the East is awake and the time has come for the world to tremble.

The fields of the final war

Just as the Imperial forces are drawn to the Rebel base, the armies of the world will be drawn to Israel. The fallen Prince will send his devils to draw them to the killing fields of Armageddon: "The spirits of devils...go forth unto the kings of the earth and of the whole world, to gather them to the battle of that great day...And he gathered them together into a place called in the Hebrew tongue Armageddon" (Revelation 16:14-16).

In 1886 the great Bible scholar, G. H. Pember, said, "Four rebel angels, and a vast number of their subordinates, are even now bound at the Euphrates, there to await the blast of the Sixth Trumpet, when the command shall be given to loose them and let them go on their errand of destruction."

It is very interesting that the space age finds some skeptics calling the Bible an out-of-date book. It has injected a new word into our space age vocabulary. A new standard dictionary defines Armageddon as "The place of a great and final conflict between the forces of good and evil." When General MacArthur, General Eisenhower, *The London Times,* and *Time Magazine* desire a word to describe an atomic holocaust, they reach back into Revelation 16:16 and use the word "Armageddon."

In June 1967, the prestigious *London Times* published an editorial on the subject of Armageddon. It identified the time, place, and participants of the war in accord with Bible prophesy.

Armageddon (also referred to as Megiddo and the Valley of Jehoshaphat), was allegedly praised by Napoleon Bonaparte as "the most ideal place on earth for military battle."

Robert L. McCan wrote in *Vision of Victory,* "Armageddon is the oldest battlefield in recorded history." And it is here, where the first recorded battle took place, that the last battle will also be fought.

Lester Velie wrote a feature article in the November, 1968 *Reader's Digest* entitled "Countdown in the Holy Land." Mr. Velie said if we're listening, we can hear it, like the dramatic voice of a man at the space center counting backwards toward a great historic event: 10...9...8...7. If you are listening, Mr. Velie said, you can hear it in the Middle East; the countdown to a catastrophic war. Mr. Velie closed his article with this sentence: "And the Middle East, which gave birth to three major world religions, could become the burial ground of civilization." The Bible says Mr. Velie is right. Here in the Middle East, where the human race was born, it will also die. Where the human race was cradled, it will also be buried—on the Plains of Armageddon.

On the Plains of Megiddo where the first recorded war of mankind was fought, the fallen Prince will draw mankind to its last war.

Dr. Jess Moody, a Christian author, said, "Perhaps even now the little flowers are blooming on the Plains of Armageddon for the last time."

The Phantom unleashes the weapons of mass destruction

It was the beginning of the *Star Wars* movies. War drums echo through the universe. They were calling forth the Empire's gigantic war machine. The thunder of death echoes through the universe. The Emperor's mighty military force is unleashed.

As in *Star Wars*, a mighty military will one day be unleashed upon mankind. This war will thrill the Devil by killing one-third of all humans in sixty minutes of human history: "And the four angels were loosed, which were prepared for an hour, and a day, and a month, and a year, for to slay the third part of men" (Revelation 9:15). The scripture says the blood will run up to the horses' bridles in the streets of Jerusalem (Revelation 14:20).

In a ghastly portrayal of the world's last war, John wrote in Revelation 19:17, 18, "And I saw an angel standing in the sun; and he cried with a loud voice, saying to all the

fowls that fly in the midst of heaven, "Come and gather your-selves together unto the supper of the great God; That you may eat the flesh of kings, and the flesh of captains, and the flesh of mighty men, and the flesh of horses, and of them that sit on them, and the flesh of all men, both free and bond, both small and great."

When John penned the Book of Revelation, the death of one-third of the human race in sixty minutes was inconceivable if not totally impossible. But today, the world has weapons capable of wiping out the entire human race within an hour.

Prepare for war

Star Wars is about war—about hatred, fighting and killing. The Bible tells us to prepare for wars that will mark our planet's future:

- Luke 21:10,11 "Nation shall rise against nation, and kingdom against kingdom."
- Revelation 11: 7 says, "The beast shall make war."
- Revelation 12:7 states, "There was war in heaven."
- Revelation 12:17 repeats, "To make war with the remnant."
- Revelation 13:4 asks, "Who is able to make war with the beast?"
- Revelation 13:7 says the devil will, "Make war with the saints."
- Revelation 17:14 says, Satan will, "make war with the Lamb."
- Revelation 19:11 says, "He does judge and make war."
- And Revelation 19:19 tells us, "Kings gathered to make war."

We have been well warned that the last days will be marked by military conflicts.

Even now, we are engaged in a spiritual war with the dark Force. War is a time for soldiers, discipline, and courage. It is a time to fight. Look at the soldiers on the drill field or in the barracks. They laugh, they joke, and sometimes they loaf. But look again at the same men on the battlefront. There is no laughter or loafing here. What is the difference? They can see the enemy. On a rising tide of evil, Satan is moving out in the open. Christians see the enemy. Paul said to Timothy, "Endure hardness, as a good soldier of Jesus Christ. No man that wars entangles himself with the affairs of this life" (II Timothy 2: 3,4).

All out! That is it. People must completely yield themselves to the Lord and daily trust in His power. Paul said words that need to echo in our minds every day: "My brethren, be strong in the Lord, and in the power of his might. Put on the whole armor of God, that you may be able to stand against the wiles of the devil. For we wrestle not against flesh and blood, but against powers, against the rulers of the darkness of this world, against spiritual wickedness in high places. Wherefore take unto you the whole armor of God, that you may be able to withstand in the evil day, and having done all, so stand" (Ephesians 6:10-13).

War with the Devil offers us a unique opportunity to glorify our Lord and achieve greatness. England rose to her greatest, most glorious hour as she saw Hitler's armies moving to destroy her. May the words of Sir Winston Churchill move us as they did the English in their hour of destiny. "Still, if you will not fight for the right when you can easily win without bloodshed; if you will not fight when your victory will be sure and not too costly, you may come to the moment when you will have to fight with all the odds against you and

only a precarious chance of survival. There may even be a worse case. You may have to fight when there is no hope of victory, because it is better to perish than live as slaves."

The uniforms are gone, but the same forces of hell are marching against Christendom today. Luke Skywalker was a hero that chose to fight rather than live as a slave of the Empire. May we make the same choice.

*Against the back drop of a full-moon sky, awe inspiring fire-
works explode. The universe vibrates with happiness. Search
lights beam the good news across the night sky. It is the celebration of the birth of a new world. It is the jubilation of the
victory of the good Force. The day of Star Wars has ended
and the day of peace has begun.*

Chapter 19
THE GREATEST VICTORY

Victory can come in the darkest hour. As the *Star Wars* battles, which began with *The Phantom Menace*, move to their
close, everything appears lost. The good droid, Artoo, is hit by
a large explosion sending smoke spurting out of the nozzles in
his body. Luke, the only hope, has gone away, and is held
prisoner on the evil ship Death Star. The wicked Emperor
tells Luke that his friends on the Sanctuary Moon are walking
into a trap. Through a round window behind the Emperor's
throne Luke can see the flashes of the space war his Rebels
are losing. He sees his force's space ships explode against the
Empire's protective shield. They cannot penetrate it. Then he
watches in horror as a powerful light from the Death Star
blows a Rebel cruiser to dust. The entire Rebel fleet is being
wiped out.

    The Emperor tells his prisoner Luke, "Your fleet is

lost. And your friends on the Endor moon will not survive. There is no escape, my young apprentice. The alliance will die...as will your friends." Luke makes a last desperate attempt to escape, but is knocked down by lightning from the Emperor's fingers. He lies writhing in pain on the floor as the thunderbolts fly from the evil hands. It appears Luke is finished, the Rebel fleet is doomed and the hope of victory over the evil Force is lost.

Suddenly everything is reversed. The huge protective shield generator protecting the Emperor explodes. Han and the rebel fighters run out of the bunker and race for their ships. Red Group, Gold Group, the Falcon and several smaller Rebel fighters come racing through space toward the Death Star. The Rebel invaders fly across the surface of the man-made planet. An Imperial Destroyer is hit by a Rebel ship and wrecked. It crashes into Death Star. For the first time the Emperor's giant ship is rocked by explosions. The Rebel fleet zooms overhead, unloading a heavy barrage of explosives. Luke jumps in an Imperial shuttle and rockets away from Death Star, just before it meets its fate. Luke has returned leading a triumphant Rebel army.

Likewise the Bible teaches that the world will go through dark days. Jesus, mankind's only hope has gone away. Armageddon will ravage the earth. Earthquakes will explode. The sea will turn to blood. All the fish will die. The grass and a third of earth's trees will be burned up. The sun and moon will be darkened. Men will gnaw their tongues for pain. Lightning and thunder will jar the earth. A giant hail storm will rain death down upon helpless masses. And one third of all humans on earth will die within sixty minutes of Armageddon's appalling battle: "And the four angels were loosed, which were prepared for an hour, and a day, and a month, and a year, for to slay the third part of men" (Revelation 9:15). It will appear all is lost. The earth seems doomed and faith of victory over the evil Force is dying.

Suddenly everything is reverse. Just when hope has gone, and the city of Jerusalem is devastated, Jesus shall return: "For I will gather all nations against Jerusalem to battle; and the city shall be taken, and the houses rifled, and the women ravished; and half of the city shall go forth into captivity, and the residue of the people shall not be cut off from the city. Then shall the Lord go forth, and fight against those nations, as when he fought in the day of battle" (Zechariah 14:1-3).

In the darkest hours of Armageddon, when it appears the Antichrist has won, Christ appears in the clouds upon the white horse of the victor. Following Him will be an army that will turn the tide against evil: "And I saw heaven opened, and behold a white horse; and he that sat upon him was called Faithful and True, and in righteousness he does judge and make war. His eyes were as a flame of fire, and on his head were many crowns; and he had a name written, that no man knew, but he himself. And he was clothed with a vesture dipped in blood: and his name is called The Word of God. And the armies which were in heaven followed him upon white horses, clothed in fine linen, white and clean. And out of his mouth goes a sharp sword, that with it he should smite the nations: and he shall rule them with a rod of iron: and he treads the winepress of the fierceness and wrath of Almighty God. And he has on his vesture and on his thigh a name written, KING OF KINGS, AND LORD OF LORDS" (Revelation 19:11-16).

Men, blinded by sin and deceived by demons, will join in a war against God. It will be the greatest struggle between the good Force and the evil Force. Jesus Christ will come to make war against the forces of evil and bring justice

to mankind: "He doth judge and make war" (Revelation 19:11).

The good Force wins

At the surprising end of the *Star Wars* series, the Jedi came rushing in through space in time to defeat the evil Imperial forces. The outcome is swift and decisive.

Likewise earth's forces of evil will fold. The Lord's army will come rushing in through space in time to defeat the evil Satanic forces: "These shall make war with the Lamb, and the Lamb shall overcome them for he is Lord of lords and King of kings: and they that are with him are called and chosen, and faithful" (Revelation 17:14). The outcome is swift and decisive.

In the end of both the fantasy world's war and the present world's Armageddon, the good Force wins.

Christ's great kingdom shall come on earth to rule forever: Then shall the King, "Set up a kingdom, which shall never be destroyed: and the kingdom shall not be left to other people, but it shall break in pieces and consume all these kingdoms, and it shall stand for ever. Forasmuch as you sawest that the stone was cut out of the mountain without hands, and that it break in pieces the iron, the brass, the clay, the silver, and the gold" (Daniel 2:44-45).

Like a giant wrecking ball the Kingdom of God will destroy all of the wicked world systems of Devil-driven men.

The evil Force is cast into a bottomless pit

With one final burst of his once-awesome strength, Darth Vader turns against the Emperor and hurls him into a bottomless shaft. His evil body goes spinning down, down, down into the endless void.

Likewise the Devil will be thrown into a bottomless

pit: "And I saw an angel come down from heaven, having the key of the bottomless pit and a great chain in his hand. And he laid hold on the dragon, that old serpent, which is the Devil, and Satan, and bound him a thousand years, And cast him into the bottomless pit, and shut him up, and set a seal upon him" (Revelation 20:1-3).

As Satan was allowed to tempt Adam and Eve in the garden, and man on earth, he must now come out to test those who have lived through the thousand years of peace on earth: "He should deceive the nations no more till the thousand years should be fulfilled and after that he must be loosed a little season" (Revelation 20:3). They may choose between Satan and the Savior.

Those that resist the Devil's final efforts to seduce them will prove their love for the Lord. This is what God created them for. Love is what only creatures with a free will to choose can give Him. So, the Devil is released to try the hearts of men one more time. He will be allowed to see how many people he can deceive and turn against the Lord.

Finally, Satan's purpose will be finished. The hearts of men will be revealed. Then, "The devil that deceived them was cast into the lake of fire and brimstone" (Revelation 20:10). Likewise, the angels that joined Satan in his rebellion against God in heaven will also be put into this prison: "And the angels which kept not their first estate, but left their own habitation, he has reserved in everlasting chains under darkness unto the judgment of the great day. Even as Sodom and Gomorrha, and the cities about them in like manner, giving themselves over to fornication, and going after strange flesh, are set forth for an example, suffering the vengeance of eternal fire" (Jude 1:6-7).

The struggle that began in heaven thousand of years before finally comes to an end. The Evil Phantom who led the rebellion in heaven and the angels who followed him are disposed of forever. Never again will they tempt, taunt or terrorize human beings.

A cleansing by fire

Fire purges impurities from silver. Fire will also purge away evil. In the end of the Special Edition of *Return of the Jedi*, Luke sets fire to a stack of logs under a funeral pyre. On top of it lies Darth Vader's evil armor; his dark mask, hellish helmet, and corrupt cape. Luke watches with remorse as the flames leap higher and higher, consuming what is left of the man who was deceived by the dark Force. The fire purges the universe's symbols of evil.

Even so, the last symbols of earth's evil must be put away and the world purged by fire: "But the day of the Lord will come as a thief in the night; in the which the heavens shall pass away with a great noise, and the elements shall melt with fervent heat, the earth also and the works that are therein shall be burned up" (II Peter 3:10).

Just as the *Star Wars* victors can stop their fighting and begin building a new peaceful world, so God will create a magnificent, new heaven and earth: "And I saw a new heaven and a new earth: for the first heaven and the first earth were passed away; and there was no more sea. And I John saw the holy city, new Jerusalem, coming down from God out of heaven, prepared as a bride adorned for her husband. And I heard a great voice out of heaven saying, Behold, the tabernacle of God is with men, and he will dwell with them, and they shall be his people, and God himself shall be with them, and be their God. And God shall wipe away all tears from their eyes; and there shall be no more death, neither sorrow, nor crying, neither shall there be any more pain: for the former things are passed away. And he that sat upon the throne said,

Behold, I make all things new. And he said unto me, Write: for these words are true and faithful. And he said unto me, It is done. I am Alpha and Omega, the beginning and the end. I will give unto him that is athirst of the fountain of the water of life freely" (Revelation 21:1-6).

The grand close

Friends and love ones are reunited in the grand ending of *Star Wars*. Hundreds of citizens gather in the streets to celebrate. A skyhopper ship flies between buildings, sending confetti raining down upon the happy crowd. Against the backdrop of a full-moon sky, awe inspiring fireworks explode. The universe vibrates with their happiness. Search lights beam the good news across the night sky. It is the celebration of the birth of a new world. It is the jubilation of the victory of the good Force. The dark night of *Star Wars* has ended and the day of peace has begun.

Some day the future will see the saints of all the ages reunite in the grand close of earth's conflicts. Millions will gather on streets of gold to celebrate. Angels will fly through the mansion of glory, sending joy raining down upon the happy crowd. Against the backdrop of a full-bright sky, awe inspiring praise will explode. The universe will vibrate with their happiness. The light of the Lamb will beam the good news across a sky which shall never see night. It is the celebration of the birth of a new world. It is the jubilation of the victory of our God. The day of earth's wars will have ended and the day of peace will begin.

"And a voice came out of the throne, saying, Praise our God, all you his servants, and you that fear him, both small and great. And I heard as it were the voice of a great multitude, and as the voice of many waters, and as the voice of mighty thunderings, saying, Alleluia: for the Lord God omnipotent reigns. Let us be glad and rejoice, and give honor to him" (Revelation 19:5-7).

END NOTES

1 *Time*, April 26, 1999, p. 92.

2 Laurent Bouzereau, *Star Wars: The Annotated Screenplays*, [Ballantine Books, New York], pp. 35, 36, 91.

3 *Time*, April 26, 1999, p. 89.

4 *Time*, Feb. 8, 1988.

5 *Time*, April 26, 1999, p. 86.

6 *The Ultimate Evil*, Maury Terry, [Doubleday & Company, Inc., Garden City, N.Y.] , p. 16.

7 Laurent Bouzereau, *Star Wars: The Annotated Screenplays*, [Ballantine Books, New York], pp. 34, 91.

8 Laurent Bouzereau, *Star Wars: The Annotated Screenplays* [Ballantine Books, New York], p. 284.

9 Laurent Bouzereau, *Star Wars: The Annotated Screenplays*, [Ballantine Books, New York] p. 182.

10 *Associated Press*, September 7, 1989.

11 Anton Szandor LaVey, "*The Satanic Bible*," [Avon Books, NY] 1969, p. 135.

12 Dave Breese, *His Infernal Majesty*, [The Moody Bible Institute, Chicago, Ill.] 1974, p. 31.

13 Cris Wood, *Macleans*, March 30, 1987, p. 54.

14 Ted Schwarz & Duane Empey, *Satanism*, [Zondervan Books, Grand Rapids, Michigan], 1988, p. 7.

15 *Atlanta Constitution*, June 9, 1988, pp. 1, 6B.

16 *Moody Monthly*, 89-03, p. 19-24.

17 *Insight*, 88-01-11, p. 48.

18 Laurent Bouzereau, *Star Wars: The Annotated Screenplays*, [Ballantine Books, New York] p.31.

19 Laurent Bouzereau, *Star Wars: The Annotated Screenplays*, [Ballantine Books, New York] p. 12.

20 Erwin W. Lutzer & John F. DeVries, *Satan's Evangelistic Strategy For This New Age* [Victor Books,]1989, p. 25.

21 Dean Halverson, "A Matter of Course: Conversation with Kenneth Wapnick," *Spiritual Counterfeits Project Journal 7*, no. 1, 1987, p.23.

22 David Spangler, *Emergence: Rebirth of the Sacred*, [Findhorn publications, n.d., Forres, Scotland] p. 144, cited in *Understanding the New Age*, p. 288.)

23 *Inside the New Age Nightmare*, Randall N. Baer, [Huntington House, Inc., Lafayette, Louisiana], 1989, p.84.

24 Christopher Lasch, *Soul of a New Ager*, "Omni," October 1987, p. 84.

25 Russell Chandler, *Understanding the New Age*, [Word Publishers, Dallas], 1988, p. 67.

26 Dave Breese, *Satan's Ten Most Believable Lies*, [Moody Press, Chicago], pp. 8, 14.

27 Laurent Bouzereau, *Star Wars: The Annotated Screenplays*, [Ballantine Books, New York] p. 267.

28 Laurent Bouzereau, *Star Wars: The Annotated Screenplays*, [Ballantine Books, New York] p. 214.

29 *Hamlet*, Act III.

30 Marx, Karl, *Des Verzweiflenden Gebet*, p. 30.

31 *Associated Press*, April 21, 1999.

32 Flood, M., "Devil Worship: What's Behind It?" *Houston Post*, September 15, 1985.

33 *USA Today*, September 27, 1989.

34 Larson, Bob, *Satanism: The Seduction of America's Youth* [Thomas Nelson, Nashville] 1989, p. 25.

35 *Newsweek*, October 16, 1989, p. 23.

36 Ed Kiersh, *Spin,* August 1988, p. 23.

37 *Insight*, January 11, 1989.

38 L. E. Maxwell, *Born Crucified*, [Moody Press, Chicago] p. 60.

39 Paul McGuire, *Evangelizing The New Age*, [Servant Publications, Ann Arbor, Michigan,] 1989, p. 104.

40 *U. S. News & World Report*, September 3, 1973.

41 *Josephus*, Book I, Chapter 6.